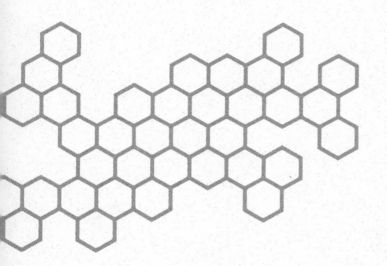

THE BEE MAKER

MOBI WARREN

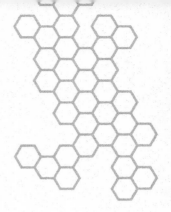

In loving memory

Mom and Dora
who cherished all creatures

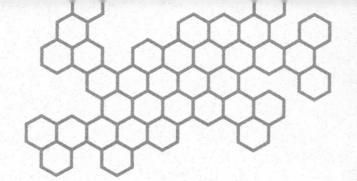

Acknowledgement for use of poem:

"A fish does not drown in water," by Mechtild
of Magdeburg, translation © 1994 Jane Hirshfield.
From **Women in Praise of the Sacred: 43
Centuries of Spiritual Poetry by Women**
(NY: HarperCollins, 1994); used by permission
of Jane Hirshfield, all rights reserved.

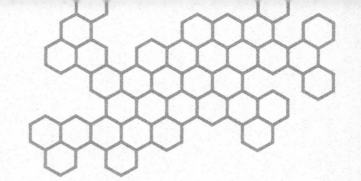

CHAPTER ONE

HONEYBEE THIEVES

Yolo County, California; 2036

Melissa and her father leaned their bikes against a fence post and silently dropped to the ground. Inch by careful inch, they belly crawled beneath the lowest rung of barbed wire. Melissa imagined herself flat as a piece of paper and didn't dare breathe until she was safely on the other side. They entered the almond orchard, one of California's last, a sea of wilting, honey-scented blossoms. Melissa stood up, inhaled the fragrance, and looked around.

To the West, the sun cast a rosy glow over a pod of clouds. Like sky dolphins, thought Melissa, then frowned. Her absent mother might be watching real dolphins off the coast of Crete right now. Well, best not to dwell on that. It was one of many things she couldn't change.

The evening air was clammy, made worse by the snug jacket and veiled helmet her father insisted she wear. Even

Hermes, her small black dog, was zipped into a protective vest. While her father prepared a smoker to calm the bees, Melissa listened to their soft thrumming. Hermes sat beside her on quivering haunches, ears pricked upward, and sniffed the air as it filled with the resiny scent of burning pine needles. Tendrils of smoke, like ghostly moths, curled and vanished in the dusky spaces between trees.

Her father hadn't wanted her to join his bee stealing heist, but he'd been too tired to argue.

"You never want me along, Ba," she'd protested.

"That's not true."

"You're mad that Mom dumped me on you."

"Don't be ridiculous. If you come, you'll have to suit up."

"Okay!""

"And stay out of the way. The bees might be aggressive."

In the way. She knew that's how Ba, her father, saw her ever since her mother left for Crete and left Melissa in his care. But she was thirteen. She could help him in his work if he'd only let her.

Now in the orchard as she bent over the stacked crates that housed the bees, her father warned, "Move back, Melissa. I need room."

His words felt like a rebuke. She moved several yards away, wriggled her gloves off and pulled a piece of origami paper from her jacket pocket. If he wasn't going to let her do anything, she might as well fold something. An origami bee. She'd been thinking of folding a thousand of them, like a secret prayer for the bees' survival, and when she was finished, giving them to her father. Maybe then he'd open up and accept her as an ally in the fight for honeybees.

She made a few base folds on the patterned yellow paper and was about to make a new crease when a thin, reedy sound, distinct from the bees, vibrated in her ear. She felt a vague, unsettling feeling that someone else was nearby. She quickly glanced around, but there was nothing to see but her father, Hermes, and the monotonous rows of almond trees. She clapped a hand against her ear, fearing a thirsty mosquito had squeezed its way through her veil. Honeybees were nearly extinct. Large, aggressive mosquitoes were not. But the rising sound took on the shape of a human song. Flute? Bagpipe? The tune was exotic, sinuous as a snake moving across water. There was a haunting sorrow in it that held Melissa half spellbound, half uneasy.

Suddenly, her father's face was only inches from her own. Hermes snuggled against her leg, whining.

"Melissa, Mel! Can you hear me?" Her father had removed his veil and she was surprised to find her own was off, as well.

"It stopped," she said blankly.

"What has?" her father asked.

"The flute or whatever was making that music."

"What music, Melissa?" Her father looked at her perplexed. "We're the only ones in the orchard."

Seeing the look in his eyes, Melissa realized that he hadn't heard any music. A slight chill raced down her spine.

"A seizure," her father said.

"That's impossible!" She hadn't had recurring absence seizures, episodes of lapsed awareness and staring spells, for several months. It couldn't have been. At her last check-up, her doctor said there was an excellent chance she had finally outgrown her epilepsy.

"Melissa, you were clearly blanked out."

She couldn't tell if he was concerned or just annoyed.

She shook her head. "I didn't blank out. I heard music." She immediately regretted saying it.

"Melissa, there was no music. You may have had a pre-seizure aura."

Melissa knew that some epileptics, like her own grandmother, heard sounds or smelled things that weren't really there, but that had never happened to her.

"We took you off meds too soon."

"I'm not going back on meds, Ba. They just made things worse." Of course, she knew that the meds had reduced her staring spells and helped with school, but she hated the side effects. Nausea, headache, dizziness.

Her father shrugged his shoulders. He hated arguments. "Honeybee, we'll keep an eye on this, okay?"

"Don't call me honeybee."

"You never objected to that nickname before."

"Well, I'm older now, Ba, and anyway, it's depressing with all the bees dying." She didn't add that he seemed to care more about bees than his own daughter. Of course, she cared about the bees, too, and now her father would think she didn't.

"Was I out long?"

"I don't think so. Fifteen, twenty seconds maybe. Hermes came and got me."

Melissa didn't contradict her father, but she was sure the music had lasted longer than twenty seconds. She reached down to pat Hermes. He was a shelter dog she'd adopted, a mixed breed that looked like a toy black Lab with the short, blunt tail of a terrier. His personality was pure Jack Russell, headstrong and stubborn. He was also sensitive to her seizures, alerting her parents whenever she had one.

Melissa noticed that her father had already placed the pale blue boxes of the beehive into a large mesh sack. He'd need to lift and then lower the hive carefully over the barbed wire fence. As he sealed the sack, he said, "I should have given you something to do instead of just standing there." They both knew she was less likely to suffer a seizure when she was physically active.

She remembered then that she had, in fact, been folding an origami honeybee while her father smoked the hive. She could still feel the slip of folded paper tucked in her half-closed fist. She opened her hand and there an origami bee sat, small and complete. That was weird. She was sure she had only started the base folds when the strange music distracted her. Yet there a finished bee sat. It was a new pattern she was proud of. She had tweaked a well known origamist's design with a few touches of her own to create a honeybee a little more than an inch long, its wings spread open and legs dangling as if it were hovering over a flower.

Her father looked down at the bee and then at her again. His eyes questioned hers.

"I was working on this before, before I blanked out."

"You took your gloves off?"

"I was bored, Ba."

To her surprise, the sharp look in his eyes turned to admiration. "That's a great design, quite elegant."

I really could fold a thousand, she thought. Dr. Paul Bùi, her father, was a research scientist who specialized in honeybee communication. He was doing everything he could think of, including stealing this hive, to prevent the final extinction of honeybees. Of course, Melissa knew folding a bunch of paper bees wouldn't bring the real ones back, but it might show her father how much she cared about his efforts. Folding them would be a prayer, a way to hold on to hope, and a way to reach her father.

She tucked the bee in her jacket pocket and helped her father hoist the hive over the fence. They crawled back beneath it.

"What if we get caught, Ba?" Melissa asked as she stood up.

"We won't. If the owner knew the packers had missed a hive, he'd have an armed guard out here and I would never have brought you."

A shiver went up Melissa's spine. She knew as well as her father that no one would relinquish a living hive, not when it could make a hefty profit on the black market or provide one last season of almonds. Almonds, so rare now, they cost several hundred dollars a pound. They strapped the hive onto her father's bicycle trailer, then folded their jackets and stuffed them in his daypack. Before they hopped on their bikes, her father turned towards her and asked, "You okay for the ride back?"

"I feel perfectly normal, Ba," she said even though she didn't at all. She still felt the vague troubling sensation she'd felt in the orchard, as if her nerves had moved out of their normal grooves, as if someone had been watching her from the shadows of the trees. And that strange music. It was unlike any seizure she'd ever had before. She pulled her bike helmet on and nodded to her father after lifting Hermes into his handlebar basket.

"We can take it slow," her father said.

"I'm okay, Ba. Really."

They straddled their bikes and started pedaling, waiting until they were well past the orchard to turn on flashing safety lights. Not that it mattered. If any driverless car, the only type allowed on main roads, passed them, its sensors would detect their bikes to avoid a collision. A rain drone whirred overhead and Melissa looked up. The silver-green drone was headed towards her dolphin clouds. It would seed them and maybe there would be light rainfall later that evening. But probably not. The drones did not have a great record of success.

As they cruised side by side, drenched in the reds and golds of a sunset sky, her father's voice rose above the bikes' soft glide. "It was a lucky break finding that hive."

Melissa knew her father had spent weeks sneaking into orchards looking for surviving honeybees. Then today when she'd returned from school, she'd found him excited and ready to take off on his bike. "I found a colony," he'd simply stated.

Now, as she gazed at both sides of the road, she saw nothing but acre after acre of parched and dying almond trees. Irrigation wells dug decades ago had no more water to give. The reign of the almond orchards was over; the honeybees all dead or disappearing.

"They used to ship bees in, right, Ba? To pollinate the almond trees?"

"Yes, from all over the world, from anywhere bees could still be found. It still makes me angry."

For decades, billions of bees had been transported like prison crews. Stressed out. Plagued by mites and prone to viruses. Exposed to now-outlawed pesticides. Pesticides, her father had explained, that damaged memory cells in their brains so badly, many bees couldn't remember the way back to their hives. There had been great hopes that after the pesticides were banned, the bees would rebound. And for some years they did, but something had changed. The bees were weaker. They no longer thrived. They began to abandon their hives again.

Melissa's absence seizures resulted in gaps of memory, small parcels of time stolen from her. It would be terrifying to forget essential things like how to find her way home, like a lost and damaged bee.

They paused on a hilltop to watch the last sliver of sun dissolve on the horizon beneath sinking layers of tangerine and turquoise sky. Overhead, the sky deepened to royal blue. A first star appeared, then another. Passage of light pollution laws before she was born meant Melissa had always known starry skies, and she could locate and name most constellations.

She turned to her father. "Ba, if the honeybees don't make it, will we?"

He didn't answer at once, as if choosing his words with care, then repeated what Melissa already knew. "They helped us pollinate crops for ten thousand years, Melissa. We've lost a lot of foods."

What chance did honeybees have, she wondered. Or humans? She could barely remember the taste of some fruits and vegetables. A good many others she'd never even tasted. Like strawberries. She'd always wanted to taste real strawberries, not the vitamin lozenges that accompanied every meal and supposedly came in flavors like strawberry or kiwi or pumpkin. She'd looked up photos of grocery aisles from twenty years ago on a holo-vid once and been amazed to see bins and shelves stuffed with foods, colors and shapes she'd never known. What she did know was the monotony of peanut butter and bread, rice and beans. Day after day after day. Meals without color.

As her eyes adjusted to the darkening skies, she began to pick out one star after another then reached over to scratch Hermes on the neck. He shifted to expose his abdomen hoping for a belly rub. She obliged him. The rain drone that had passed over earlier zigzagged in the distance aglitter with small lights, still in search of promising clouds like some sleek mammal seeking a mate.

"You can't snuggle with bees the way you do with a dog," her father said, "but they were every bit as loyal."

Melissa leaned over and kissed the top of Hermes' smooth, black head.

Her father kicked a stone at the side of the road and gripped his handlebars. A salt-scented breeze blew in from the Pacific and ruffled Melissa's hair as a last, thin beam of sunlight shot in an arc from the horizon as if Melissa were its target. For an instant, a lock of her brown-black hair that fell across her eyes danced with red sparkles. She glanced up at the night sky deepening to indigo. The Milky Way revealed itself like a river of white bees stretched across the heavens. Melissa felt as if she could reach up and scoop a handful. If only the stars were actual bees, she thought, I would gather them and give them back to the world. Magically bring them back. Eat a bowl of strawberries everyday. Make things better with Ba.

Her father leaned over his handlebars and before coasting down the hill, said in a low but resolute voice, "I will do everything I can to pull honeybees back from the brink of extinction. Texas, here we come!"

And I'll fold a thousand origami bees, Melissa resolved. But why Texas? If only it wasn't Texas! Far away, steaming hot, unfamiliar Texas. She knew that the next morning, they would clamp their bikes onto a rented solar van rigged to transport the beehive as well as a modest collection of belongings and leave Yolo County, California forever. Her father had mentioned there was an old-fashioned furniture maker in the town they were going to and he planned on buying a pair of rocking chairs crafted from mesquite wood as soon as they were settled. Melissa frowned at the thought. Rocking back and forth on a porch might be her father's idea of relaxing. Personally, she preferred going for a run. She and her mother used to jog together and Melissa was always seizure free on runs. Her father never joined them. He'd never even bothered going to one of Melissa's cross-country meets.

They'd be crossing the wide, arid desert, the infamous Hell Zone, to reach Texas. Just the two of them, since her parents were divorced and her archeologist mother, on a dig in Crete, wouldn't be stateside any time soon. Their destination was the little town of Benefit, home to Benefit College, where her father had accepted a new post. He hadn't bothered to consult Melissa about the move, simply announced it one evening after another colorless dinner. When she protested, he refused to listen. He left the dinner table for his study, leaving a tearful Melissa to wash up. It had seemed monstrously unfair. Another thing she had no power to change.

The next evening, perhaps in an effort to soften the blow, he'd told her the town was tucked at the foot of a limestone canyon along the curve of the Sabinal River in the heart of Texas Hill Country. "It's a lovely town," he said, "one of the first in Texas to go off the grid, years before Climate Chaos forced everyone else to. I've rented a little house with a wrap around porch and our next-door neighbors have a small goat farm. That'll be interesting, don't you think? I understand a thirteen-year-old boy lives there."

"Great," Melissa had retorted, "he probably smells like a goat."

CHAPTER TWO

GOAT BOY

Dia, Crete; Sixth Century BCE

Amethea, with the help of the slave Dika, cleansed her mother's body with olive oil before wrapping it in a garment of clean white wool. She combed her mother's hair and tied the copper curls with an embroidered violet band. It had been her mother's favorite ornament, a gift earned when she ran the famed Heraea footrace at age sixteen. Dika swept the house and Amethea hung a funerary wreath braided from wild celery leaves on the wall.

The two women stood at the foot of the deathbed. Dika intoned a lament while Amethea played her aulos, a double flute with reeds for mouthpieces. Amethea, tall and lean, with her own unruly mass of red curls, did her best to maintain composure for the sake of her nine-year-old brother Hippasus. He huddled, his bad foot curled beneath the stool he sat on. His right leg ended in a stump that resembled a hoof more than a human foot and two odd bumps protruded from his head like the stunted horns of a goat. He buried his tear-stained face in the smooth fur of their fawn-colored hound Dove who stood close to him on long, thin legs.

Dove's ears pricked and she whined in a low voice to announce the arrival of the siblings' uncle Karpos. A broad shoul- dered man with jutting jaw and dark beard brusquely entered the room. His embroidered tunic was gathered loosely at the waist with a gold belt. With a hand gesture that signaled impa- tience, he cut off Dika's chanting and motioned to her husband Kimon, standing in the doorway behind him, to carry the body to a cart outside. When Karpos noticed Hippasus in the corner, he grunted, "Out!"

The boy, with a sudden look of fright in his pale blue eyes, grabbed the cane tucked beneath the stool and planted it on the earthen floor. He placed his other hand on Dove's firm haunches as he stood and shuffled from the room. Dove accompanied him, the curl of her tail tucked between her legs.

Karpos roared, "Hide yourself, bastard, and for your own safety, do not follow us to the pyre!"

Amethea winced but held her tongue. Her uncle had never accepted her brother. While her mother lay dying, he had even cruelly suggested that Hippasus, "an abomination to the gods," was the cause of fever that had killed dozens of Dia villagers in recent weeks.

After the cremation, Amethea would climb the hill behind their cottage to find Hippasus and do her best to comfort him. She knew she would find him at the ruined shrine the two of them had discovered the previous year, hidden among crum- bling boulders and thorn bushes. But for now, she lifted her aulos and played as she followed her mother's body down the rocky path to the waiting pyre. She was numb with grief.

Her uncle's eyebrows shot up when he realized she was not playing a proper dirge but a dance tune. He scowled and though Amethea felt his disapproval as sharply as if he had struck her, she continued to play her mother's favorite song. It was a graceful tune pierced now with Amethea's sorrow. She played until her mother's body was laid on the pyre and then stood silently as bright tongues of fire consumed it. The air filled with the acrid, oily stench of burning flesh despite the perfumed oils and armfuls of herbs they had tossed over the body. Amethea held her shawl over her nose and fought an urge to gag. In life, her mother had always smelled of roses, of honey and almonds.

Dika moaned and keened. As a slave, it was her duty to publicly mourn, but Amethea knew that the slave's grief was genuine. Her mother had treated Dika more like a sister than a slave and to Amethea, Dika was like a dependable, affectionate aunt.

Few others had gathered to pay their respects, but Amethea noticed that her good friend Kleis was there with her mother. They nodded at Amethea, their eyes brimming with sympathy, and Kleis' mother placed an armful of white roses by the pyre. Nearby, another funeral was taking place. Amethea glanced over at the family preparing to light a pyre on which the lifeless body of a young boy was laid. The boy's father, the local tanner, jerked his head up and shot Amethea a dark glance. It was not just her uncle, she knew. Other villagers blamed her brother for the fever.

It would be better for everyone, she realized, the sooner she and Hippasus left the small island of Dia for the main island of Crete and joined her uncle's household in the wealthy, bustling city of Larisa. The siblings' simple, rustic life on Dia was coming to an end. Dika and Kimon had fulfilled their fifteen years of servitude and were now free to go out on their own. Kimon would tend the flock of goats her mother had gifted him and the enterprising Dika was already hawking sesame seeds in the public market. Amethea knew life in Larisa would be a far cry from life on Dia and she dreaded it. In Larisa, Karpos lived in a lavish home with painted walls and mosaic floors, not at all like her mother's cottage adorned only with herbs and roses.

Amethea did not want to leave the sea-scented cliffs of Dia where she had been free to run and Hippasus had, until recently, been mostly ignored save for occasional taunts from other boys who shouted "Goat Boy!" when they saw him. The fever had changed that, though, and now villagers cast hard stares or muttered curses under their breath when they mentioned the goat-footed boy. It was no longer safe for Hippasus to remain on Dia. Unable to explain the deadly fever; villagers blamed Hippasus because he was different, deformed.

It was her uncle's legal obligation to assume guardianship of his sister's children, but the relief Amethea felt when Karpos arrived from Larisa, quickly dissipated. It was clear Karpos was repulsed by his crippled nephew, but he would have to take him in, wouldn't he?

Hours later, Amethea poured a flask of wine over her mother's ashes to cool them then watched as Kimon swept the ashes along with shards of bone into a clay urn. They lowered the urn into a hole in the earth and buried it. Though her mother was born to a high-ranking family, there was no marble stele to mark her grave, only a rudely painted wooden plaque. Amethea knew that her uncle blamed his sister for whatever misfortune befell her. He had never forgiven her for refusing to expose Hippasus, the goat boy, at birth. But Hippasus was not a satyr's son, no matter what Karpos and others claimed. Hadn't the honeybees, messengers of Artemis, appeared at his birth to welcome him?

Amethea climbed a narrow, familiar path, and made her way by starlight to the shrine where Hippasus lay next to Dove, the dog's body curved protectively about him. The shrine was tucked among jagged cliffs and concealed from easy view by an overgrown tangle of windblown acanthus bushes. Little remained of the original structure save for a sunken marble floor flanked by a pair of half-toppled columns and a rough-hewn cube of rose marble that must have once served as an altar.

Amethea and Hippasus kept the shrine a secret. They liked having a meeting place where no one else could find them. They decided the ruin was very ancient, built by a long forgotten people, especially after Hippasus lifted a loose stone in the marble floor one day and found buried there a votive figure of tarnished gold. It was unlike any object they had ever seen, a bee-headed woman with a cinched waist and billowing skirts. They cleaned and polished her, named her Bee Goddess, and gathered wild-flowers to place on the marble cube. A colony of wild honey-bees lived in a tree snag next to the shrine. Often, bees paused at the altar stone, leaving behind gold flecks of pollen, as if they, too, intended to make offerings.

Beneath a starry sky, sitting on the cracked marble floor, Amethea held Hippasus in her arms and let him weep before she lifted her aulos and played to lighten her own grief. Hippasus was just a small, innocent boy, she thought, a boy who would never have survived infancy if her uncle and her father had had their way.

After a while, Hippasus' sobs quieted, and he looked up into his sister's face. "Tell me a story, Amethea, like mother used to."

Their mother had been a gifted storyteller who entertained her children with tales of heroes and gods. Amethea thought for a moment.

"Will Atalanta do?" she asked Hippasus.

He clapped his hands. "Oh, yes, Amethea! I like that one. It makes me think of you."

Amethea laughed softly. "Well, I don't think my legs could ever be as swift as Atalanta's. But let me begin. Atalanta was raised by a great she-bear."

"Why didn't her own mother raise her?" interrupted Hippasus.

Amethea hesitated. Odd, but her brother had never asked that question. She then realized that their mother left out part of the story when she told it to Hippasus. Left it out for a reason.

"Didn't she have a human mother?" pressed Hippasus.

"Yes, but her father, King Iasus, desired a son, so when Atalanta was born, he was so angry he ordered her abandoned on a mountaintop."

"Did her mother protest?" Hippasus looked down at his foot and rubbed a hand lightly over the bumps on his head. His gestures made Amethea uneasy.

"It is a father's right to decide if a newborn lives or dies." Had Hippasus guessed the truth of his own story, wondered Amethea?

Before he could ask another question, Amethea placed her hand gently on his chest. "No more interruptions."

Hippasus nodded. "Tell me about her race with Hippomenes!"

Amethea smiled. That was her favorite part of the story, too. "Very well! After several adventures, Atalanta was reunited with her father and like all fathers, he expected her to marry, but Atalanta had no desire to be ruled by a husband. She finally agreed to marry only if a suitor could beat her in a race. If he failed, he must suffer death."

Hippasus' eyes grew round. "That was ruthless, don't you think, Amethea?"

"Yes, I suppose," answered Amethea, "but Atalanta was used to a free, unhampered life in the wild and wanted to discourage suitors. I don't think she expected so many young men to try and fail. In any case, many men lost their lives trying to win her hand. Then one day, the able Hippomenes travelled through her father's kingdom and caught a glimpse of Atalanta sprinting through the woods. His heart leapt. He had never seen a young woman so full of life. He resolved, like so many before him, to try for her hand by challenging her to a race. He knew very well that Atalanta was rumored to be the swiftest runner in all of Greece and she would be hard, if not impossible, to beat."

Amethea paused for a moment and pulled Hippasus closer to her. She thought about Atalanta's vitality and how Hippomenes had admired it even more than her beauty or her father's wealth. He had been a different kind of suitor, one who loved Atalanta for who she truly was. There are not many men like that, Amethea thought. Certainly not my uncle. Or my father.

"So what did Hippomenes do?" Hippasus squirmed against Amethea, anxious to hear the rest of the story.

Amethea gave a quick smile. She knew her brother knew the story as well as she did, but he always enjoyed a story as if hearing it for the first time.

"If he couldn't win by the power in his own legs," she continued, "he decided to win through cunning. He went to the temple of Aphrodite and beseeched her help. Moved by his ardor for Atalanta, the goddess gave him three golden apples that sparkled like little suns. She instructed him to toss them in front of Atalanta during the race to bewitch her. Hippomenes did as the goddess bade him. First one, then a second, he tossed the apples. Dazzled by their brightness, Atalanta couldn't resist chasing after them. Even so, twice she bounded back to the racetrack and overtook Hippomenes. In despair, he threw the third and last apple so far afield that by the time Atalanta fetched it and sprinted back to the race, he managed to beat her by a foot length."

Amethea's own legs tensed as she told this part of the story, feeling in her own body Atalanta's supreme effort.

"Was Atalanta upset?" asked Hippasus.

"No, I don't think so. By that time, Atalanta was tired of sending young men to their doom. And whether it was Aphrodite's spell or her own heart, Atalanta found Hippomenes a worthy mate. He had no desire to make her settle down and suffer the dull existence of a wife. He promised her they would live a free, untamed life hunting wild boar and sailing the wine dark sea in search of adventure. And so they married."

Amethea lifted her face to the starry sky. Like Atalanta before she met Hippomenes, Amethea was not keen on getting married. Sometimes she daydreamed about meeting a suitor like Hippomenes, someone who would admire and support her love of running, but she knew how unlikely, even impossible, that was.

"Did Atalanta still run after that?" piped Hippasus.

"Oh, I am sure she did. For the sheer pleasure of it."

Hippasus snuggled against her. "When I watch you run, Amethea, I can feel your joy. I run by watching you."

Amethea looked down at her crippled brother and felt a stab of pity. He would never know the joy of running in his own limbs.

"I run for the two of us, Hippasus. I carry you in my heart when I run."

"Thank you, Amethea."

She knew that Hippasus did not realize that her running days were rapidly coming to an end. She had been free to run on winding goat paths and high meadows in Dia, but at Karpos' estate on the big island, she would be expected to spend most of the day spinning and weaving with his wife and daughters, isolated in the women's quarters. That was the lot of women. The same boundaries would soon define and cramp her own life. Atalanta had raced to preserve a life of freedom. If only she could do the same! She lifted her flutes and poured her longing into her music.

CHAPTER THREE

A STATUE

Yolo County, California

Melissa and her father were almost home with their precious cargo of stolen bees.

"Why is Texas the only place you can do your work?" Melissa switched gears and huffed to get up the last steep hill. Her shortness of breath did not conceal her unhappiness over the move.

Her father stopped at the crest of the hill. "Melissa, we've already been over this. I know you don't want to leave your school and the cross country team, but—"

"It's not just that," she interrupted. "What about Noi?"

Dr. Bùi got off his bike to check on the bees and then straddled it again. "Look, I know you won't be able to hop on the solar rail to San Francisco whenever you feel like it," he admitted, "and I'll miss that, too."

Not as much as I will, Melissa thought glumly. Her father had no idea how important her visits with her grandmother had become since her mother left for Crete. There were things she could talk about with Noi that were impossible to talk about with her father. Three years earlier, her parents' divorce hadn't come as a complete surprise—after all, they had always seemed more wed to their research projects than to each other. But her mother changing custodian arrangements six months earlier had been a shock. Being able to confide in Noi had helped a little. But now Melissa and her father were moving nearly two thousand miles away. It felt way too soon to have to go through another big change.

The Milky Way draped across the dark sky like a shawl of white wool. Melissa leaned over her handlebars and buried her face in Hermes' soft fur.

"My work is in Texas now," her father said. "A team of honeybee experts has gathered at Benefit College and I need to be there. It may be the last shot we have at saving them."

What could Melissa say to that unless she wanted to sound like she didn't care about the honeybees? And she did. She knew her father's work was important. But why when she finally started to feel halfway comfortable at school, did they have to move? She'd earned a place on the cross-country team and those kids were mostly positive and supportive. Of course, things weren't perfect. She didn't have any close friends, not really. Her blank-out seizures made other kids find her weird. She knew they called her 'statue girl' behind her back. But at least everyone knew about her condition. The thought of having to face a whole new group of kids and teachers was scary.

"I know, Ba. Bees, bees, bees." She turned from him and leaned over her handlebars to speed down the last hill.

"Wait, Honeybee,"

"Ba, not that name."

She zoomed downhill, leaving her father behind, and turned a corner onto their street. After she put her bike up, she showered beneath a rainwater bag and put on an old race shirt for a nightgown. She walked barefoot to the kitchen and poured herself a glass of water when her holographic wristband chirped. She waved a finger over the screen and a small, three-dimensional image of her mother appeared.

"Mom?!"

Claire Berry's freckled face looked up at her, smiling. Her unruly, red hair, so unlike Melissa's straight, blunt cut, was pulled back in a ponytail. She wore a silver running shoe on a chain around her neck. Melissa lifted a hand to touch the identical charm around her own neck, a gift from her mother after the first race they ran together.

"Melissa! I made the most amazing find today!"

Melissa rolled her eyes. It was typical of her mother to dispense with anything like a hello-how-are-you when she was excited about some project.

"That's nice," she responded in a monotone, and then added, "So did Ba."

"Ba found something?" Her mother looked momentarily puzzled.

"A hive of bees."

"By the goddess, that's great! I know he's been searching for survivors."

Her mother's image flickered in and out of sight and Melissa could barely make out the next disjointed phrases, interrupted by static.

"...beneath a shrine...a bronze figurine..."

"Mom, the signal's breaking up. I can't hear you. You found a statue?"

The connection went dead but a few seconds later there was a flash and a holographic image lifted from the screen and hovered in the air. The 3-D image, eight inches tall, was of a small bronze figurine, a young woman holding a palm frond aloft in one hand. She wore a short tunic and her right shoulder and breast were bared. Melissa guessed she represented an ancient Greek athlete. The palm leaf would have been an emblem of victory. She suddenly understood the excitement in her mother's voice. Her mother's field of expertise was the Ancient Mediterranean with a special interest in women athletes. Melissa thought back to a conversation she'd had with her mother before Claire Berry had departed for Dia, a tiny island off the coast of Crete.

"This scrap of papyrus," her mother announced while holding up a rare fragment in gloved hands, "mentions a race between a girl and a boy on Dia twenty-six hundred years ago."

"So?" Melissa had responded.

"It's a big deal, Honeybee, because based on what we know, races in Ancient Greece were always segregated. Girls raced girls. Boys raced boys."

"What about that story you used to tell me about Atalanta and Hippomenes?" Melissa countered.

"That's different, of course. That's a myth and probably never actually happened or happened long before taboos forbade women and men to compete. Women weren't even allowed to watch the men's Olympics."

"I don't race against boys in cross-country," observed Melissa.

"True," her mother agreed, "but no one forbids you from watching the boys. And when we run in a community 5K, we all run together, right?"

"Yeah," Melissa conceded, fingering her race shoe charm.

"Well, last month a biologist studying a band of endangered kri-kri goats on Dia discovered the ruins of an ancient shrine revealed thanks to mega-storm erosion. I want to sift through that ruin and look for any relics that might offer up clues to a girl-boy race. And anyway, that island is not going to be there much longer, not with the steady creep of sea rise."

What happened next took Melissa utterly by surprise. After her mother secured permissions and assembled a top-notch research team for a dig on Dia, she suddenly and unexpectedly left Melissa in her father's care. Melissa and her father hadn't lived in the same house in over three years. He felt practically like a stranger. Melissa didn't know when she'd see her mother in person again. Melissa was interested in ancient women athletes, too, but not when they robbed her of a mother and dumped her on the doorstep of a reluctant father.

Melissa flicked a finger to turn the hologram of the statuette full circle, and to her surprise, discovered a name inscribed on the back of the girl's right heel. In happier days, her mother had taught her the Greek alphabet, as well as a lot of Greek words, so she was able to sound the name out. Amethea. In spite of herself, she felt a rush of excitement. Artists didn't normally sign their works back then. She wondered if it could be the name of the athlete. Here was an image of a girl named Amethea who had lived long ago. A runner like herself.

Melissa found her father on the back deck stargazing. A paper-thin flexible tablet balanced on one of his legs. It was covered with equations and diagrams that seemed to be writing themselves. She tapped her wristband and the hologram of the little victory statue rose in the air. "Ba, take a look at this. Mom found it on her dig."

Her father slipped his glasses, which were perched on top of his head, back down over his eyes. It was funny, Melissa thought, how he preferred old-fashioned glasses to laser correction or to tablet functions that automatically adjusted to a person's eyesight. Just about no one still wore glasses.

He examined the hologram with interest though Melissa noticed his eyes were rimmed with fatigue.

"That's quite a find; I'm happy for your Mom."

He didn't sound happy, Melissa thought, but surprised her by adding, "The girl reminds me of you, Honeybee."

"Ba, not that name,"

"Right, I keep forgetting."

Melissa plopped down in a deck chair next to her father. Her legs burned from the long bike ride, she was anxious about the move to Texas, and her feelings about her mother were a mess. On top of all that, she was frustrated, really frustrated that she'd had a seizure for the first time in months and heard music that wasn't really there. And yet, looking at the little bronze statue, she felt a flash of joy. The girl Amethea felt almost familiar, as if she could be a classmate or a fellow runner on the cross-country team.

She examined the hologram more closely. Amethea had a calm Mona Lisa smile, the kind seen on statues made during Greece's Archaic Period, an art history fact she'd learned from her mother. She wondered if Amethea's life had been less complicated than her own or filled with greater hardship. Perhaps it had been both. No fossil-fueled climate change back then but then no modern medicine either. Over twenty-six hundred years separated them but they were both runners. As she looked at the statuette, a sense of connection kindled within her. She felt part of a long line of women runners that extended far into the past and that lifted her spirits.

Melissa waved a finger over her wristband and the hologram disappeared. She searched the night sky for the backwards question mark that outlines the lion's mane in the constellation Leo. It was an easy constellation to find in the spring and summer sky, one of her favorites. Regulus, the star that marks the heart of the lion, was shining blue-white like the cap of an ocean wave. She picked up a piece of origami paper from a small stack she kept by her deck chair and began to fold a bee.

"Harmony of the spheres," her father said softly.

"What?" Melissa asked.

Her father turned to her and asked, "Do you know who Pythagoras was?"

"Sure, the guy they named the Pythagorean theorem after. The sum of the squares of the legs of a right triangle is equal to the square of the hypotenuse. A squared plus B squared equals C squared. We learned that this year."

"Exactly. Well, Pythagoras claimed the planets make a sublime music as they move in their orbits. Your mother claimed she heard it the night she and I first met."

Melissa was surprised that her energetic and fact-filled mother could have made so romantic a statement and even more surprised that her father was sharing it with her. She sat still and listened to the night sounds of crickets chirping. She didn't hear anything that might be stars singing. She turned her attention back to origami and folded her square in half diagonally. It was going to take months to fold a thousand.

"You know," her father said, "Pythagoras and honeybees share a connection. Some claim he was fed honeycomb as an infant, but there's more than that. Remember that Scottish colleague of your mother's that visited us some years ago?"

Melissa stiffened. Colin Anderson with his shock of red hair and infectious laugh had shown her photos of the small, restored castle he lived in. He was an expert at retrieving layers of hidden text from ancient scrolls. Melissa had found his Scottish brogue charming, but she had also noticed her mother exchange glances with him that suggested feelings beyond the mere friendship of colleagues. She wondered if her father had noticed.

"Not long ago," her father continued, "he published an article about a passage he uncovered by the world's first geographer, a man named Hecataeus."

"Lecture alert," Melissa warned. On occasion, her normally reticent father waxed on about arcane subjects as if she were in one of his graduate classes. It was usually annoying, as if he wasn't really speaking to her, just at her.

"Hear me out, Honeybee."

Melissa glared at him.

"I mean, Mel."

Melissa rolled her eyes. She'd heard it said that old habits die hard. Her father, eyeglasses perched on his nose, was a living example.

"The text contained a reference to Pythagoras, said he journeyed to a land called Hyperborea to visit devotees of Apollo and that he took along an urn of honeycomb from a tiny island called Dia. Here's the interesting part—Dia is where your mother is right now."

"I sort of remember Mom mentioning that. Where was Hyperborea, anyway?"

"Your mother thinks it refers to the British Isles and that Pythagoras' hosts might have been Druids."

"That's interesting, I guess," Melissa murmured, though she was only half-listening as she made her origami folds. She didn't want to talk any more about her mother, not when she could sense loneliness in her father's voice that only deepened her own. She opened the folded square of paper and folded it in half again the other direction and decided to divert the conversation to the less emotional subject of math, her favorite subject at school.

"Since Pythagoras was into math, I bet he liked how honeycombs are tessellated hexagons."

"No doubt," her father answered. "Pythagoras believed all of nature was based on Number. He knew six was the first perfect number, too, and of course, a hexagon has six sides."

"Six is my favorite number." Melissa opened the paper again and this time folded it in half horizontally.

"How come?" her father asked.

"I don't know; there's just something dependable about it. I always choose six or some multiple of six when I have to make a guess in a game or if I need a number for a password code, and I always like my race bibs to have a six in the number."

"Does it give you an advantage?"

Melissa detected a slight note of amused skepticism in her father's voice. He might enjoy thinking about things like the harmony of the spheres but he didn't approve of superstition.

She admitted, "Probably not, but it does make me feel more confident. But you said Pythagoras knew six was a perfect number? What's a perfect number?"

Her father twined his hands together. "It's a number whose divisors, not including itself, add up to the number. Tell me, what are the divisors, or factors, of six?"

"One, two, three, and six."

"Now leave off six and add up the others."

"They sum to six. Are there are a lot of perfect numbers?"

"There are, but in the time of Pythagoras, only three perfect numbers were known: six, twenty-eight, and four hundred ninety-six."

"How come you know all that?" Melissa asked.

"I'm an incorrigible geek. I thought you knew that by now."

I'd know a lot more, Melissa thought, if you bothered to speak to me more often. She turned back to her folding and began mentally tallying the factors of twenty-eight. One, two, four, seven, fourteen. They summed to twenty-eight.

"Of course, I don't think that's why bees use hexagons."

Her father was definitely more talkative than usual tonight, and Melissa found herself drawn into his reflections. "So why do they?"

"Darwin praised honeybees for being perfect engineers, and I have to agree. Turns out the hexagonal grid used by honeybees is the very best way to divide up a surface using the least amount of wax. There's even a mathematical proof for that."

"Honeybees must be pretty smart to come up with a design that conserves resources," said Melissa. Using rules of divisibility and her own agility with numbers—she was at the top of her class in math—she started to mentally list the factor pairs of four hundred ninety-six, the third perfect number. *Let's see, two and two hundred forty-eight...*

Her father, unaware of her mental gymnastics, said, "A human brain contains more than a hundred billion cells. A honeybee brain has less than a million. That's a huge difference, but bees can learn new things and solve problems. Did you know bees could be trained to recognize individual human faces? "

"That's wild. I don't think I could tell any bees apart by their faces."

Four and one hundred twenty-four. Five and six aren't factors. Okay, so eight and... It wasn't easy to figure out factors of four hundred ninety-six and pay attention to the intricate folds of her origami bee at the same time. She stopped folding and looked up at her father. "Can you?"

"Recognize bees from their faces? I sometimes think I can."

"Well, all our brain cells don't seem to make humans very smart, not when we've wiped out the bees."

Her father nodded. "It's what you do with your brain cells that counts, not how many you have."

Melissa's next fold, a reverse crimp, was delicate and required her full attention as well as nimble fingers. Once accomplished, she returned to factors. *Okay, eight and sixty-two. No nine or ten or eleven. Twelve, nope. Guess I have to jump all the way to sixteen...*

She gazed again at the star Regulus. A faint wisp of sound vibrated in her ear. Some insect, she assumed, as she figured out the final factor pair. *Sixteen and thirty-one. Now to add them all up.* It took her a couple minutes, but *there, yes, they sum to four hundred ninety-six.* She felt proud to have cracked the code of the third perfect number. Mental math always felt like a shower for her brain. It left her feeling refreshed and helped her put aside things that were bothering her. Like seizures. Or moving to Texas. Or a mother who was half way around the world.

Holding her half-completed bee in one hand, she turned to her father again. "So how come Pythagoras only figured out three perfect numbers?" She was sure Pythagoras must have been particularly brilliant, and if she, a thirteen-year-old girl, could figure out and add the factors of the third perfect number in a matter of minutes, couldn't he have done better?

"Well," her father answered, "for one thing, the kind of arithmetic you and I take for granted hadn't been invented yet. In the time of Pythagoras, everything was proved in terms of geometry. Number relationships were represented by lines or squares or series of dots like pebbles."

"If Pythagoras saw numbers as geometric shapes, he would have been a whiz at origami."

"Except for the fact that paper hadn't been invented yet. That took the genius of the Chinese some centuries later."

Melissa yawned. Hermes had followed her to the deck and was lying against her feet, softly snoring. The faint, insect-like sound Melissa had noticed earlier grew louder and more distinct until it drowned out the gentle whoosh of Hermes' snores. The dog's ears pricked ever so slightly in his sleep and his forelegs trembled as if he were having a dream. Melissa reached down to stroke his smooth black head and then jerked back upright. The sound had grown clear enough for her to make out the same haunting, sorrow-filled melody she had heard in the almond grove.

The volume steadily increased. Surely her father heard it this time. She turned to look at him but he wasn't there. She was shocked to discover she was no longer on their deck, but facing an ancient ruin with half-toppled marble columns and a floor of broken tiles. She saw this by starlight for the night sky was so thick with stars it seemed to pulsate. A brisk, cool wind carried the tang of salt. She could hear the shushed, steady pounding of waves; and scents of thyme and roses washed over her. From the distance came a goat's bleat, but it, like everything in this place, was held in the mesmerizing tune of the flute.

Two figures sat within the ruin. At first Melissa thought it was a woman sitting next to a goat but then saw it wasn't a goat at all but a small boy pouring a clutch of pebbles from one hand to the other. The older girl beside him blew softly into a pair of joined flutes. The boy leaned against her and his breath came in ragged gasps as if he had been crying. The girl put her flutes down and placed her arm around him. She was wearing a long tunic clasped at the shoulders with brooches in the shape of dolphins. A headband circled her loose, shoulder-length curly hair. Starlight pooled over the pair as if they sat in a waterfall made of light.

Then the scene dissolved and Melissa, dazed and frightened, found herself back on the deck sitting beside her father. What had just happened? Hermes, still cuddled at her feet, softly snored. His legs twitched and she could feel the rise and fall of his chest against her ankle. She turned towards her father who gazed quietly at the stars. Neither Hermes nor her father gave any indication she had blanked out. She looked down at her hands. A fully folded origami bee sat there. But she was certain she had only folded the bee halfway.

"I wonder what Pythagoras would have thought if someone handed him one of your origami bees," her father said as if unaware of any break in their conversation.

Melissa stared at the bee, confused. How did she do that? She didn't dare tell her father that she had heard the music again when clearly he hadn't, nor could she share that she'd seen two youths in a ruined shrine and had somehow completed an origami bee without being aware of it. She didn't want to believe she'd had another seizure, so unlike any she'd ever had before. This was more like a hallucination, a dream. If she told Ba, he'd insist on meds.

I'm super tired, she reasoned. I must have nodded off and dreamt about the girl with the flute. It looked like something out of Ancient Greece. Well, that made sense; seeing her Mom's statue of an ancient girl runner and Ba mentioning all that stuff about Pythagoras must have triggered it. Maybe she'd kept folding the origami bee the way some people walked in their sleep. After all, folding origami was almost a reflex with her. She closed her hand around the bee. It was real enough; the bee was no hallucination.

"Ba, I'm going to bed. I'm super tired." She stood up and stretched.

"I'm off to bed myself," he said, but instead bent his head over his tablet and resumed fiddling with his equations.

Melissa leaned down, intending to give her father a hug, but he was already lost in his own thoughts and didn't respond. Hugless, she straightened back up. For a moment she'd felt like she was having a real conversation with her father. They'd been connecting. How could he not notice she wanted to give him a hug? Her mother was a hugger but you can't hug someone when they're on the other side of the planet. Holo-vids, as amazing as they were, couldn't replicate the simple warmth and spontaneity of a human hug. Her father was right here on the porch with her, but apparently he couldn't replicate one either.

"You're going to like Benefit," he said without looking up from his tablet, "you'll see."

Without answering, she trudged off to her bedroom, bare save for a lightweight sleeping bag on the floor. Before flopping on top of it, she tapped her wristband to take one last look at the hologram of her mother's statue. Twenty-six hundred years ago a girl ran a race. Melissa looked again at the girl's name on the right heel and that's when she noticed, so faint she had missed it the first time, the outline of a honeybee like a punctuation mark after Amethea's name.

CHAPTER FOUR

RACE DREAMS

Dia, Crete

Amethea sat facing Karpos at a small round table in the inner garden of the cottage, her chest tight with anxiety. She did not look directly at him but gazed at the white roses that climbed an olivewood trellis behind him. Her mother had cared tenderly for those roses, watering them every dawn and speaking softly to them as if they were young children. Roses in full bloom the day before now hung limply on their stems. Did they miss her mother, too, she wondered?

Her own grief was so raw it burned within her like onion rubbed into a wound. Despite that, she sat erect, a calm expression on her face. Tears, she knew, would only irritate Karpos and, like it or not, she must now depend on whatever goodwill her uncle possessed. She had begun to doubt whether or not he intended to assume guardianship of Hippasus. In all her conversations with him concerning the move to Larisa, he had avoided any mention of her brother.

Amethea poured Karpos a cup of diluted wine and offered him a clay dish of figs and almonds. He gulped the wine and cleared his throat as if to speak, but when Amethea looked up, his eyes did not meet hers. Instead they moved slowly over her face and body in a way that made her feel uneasy.

At length he spoke. "You are an echo of your father."

It was, thought Amethea, an unusual way to begin a conversation. She had not seen her father in nine years, not since he divorced her mother and left Crete. Why bring him up now?

"Fire in your grey eyes, like Adelphos. Your arms are taut and sleek, as I guess your legs are." Her tunic reached to her ankles, hiding her legs, though her athletic contours were not hard to guess.

Amethea felt as though her uncle were appraising her the way he might a horse for a chariot race and it made her uncomfortable. She knew his stables in Larisa held some of the finest steeds in Crete, a fact he was fiercely proud of. Would he consider her a prize to show off, as well? She didn't know what to say so silently cast her eyes downwards.

"Like your father, you would make a fine runner."

Amethea lifted her eyes. "Mother ran a race, too," she blurted, then blushed at how quickly she had lost her composure to defend her mother.

"Yes, yes," responded Karpos, his voice edged with irritation. "Did you think I wouldn't recognize the violet headband? It was a gift from your father on the day your mother won the Heraea. I'm surprised she kept it. Perhaps she regretted her decision regarding the boy?"

"My mother rarely spoke of my father. She never spoke of regrets. She was proud of Hippasus."

"Proud of a goat-footed, goat-horned boy? Your mother, I see, persisted in her madness. Adelphos, if indeed he was the father, would not claim the monster."

"Hippasus is learning his letters, Uncle, and he can play the lyre. And no one can heal an injured animal better." Again, she knew she had spoken too passionately, but she wanted her uncle to appreciate Hippasus' good qualities.

"Heal an animal?" he retorted and spat. "Better to use his gift to keep his own mother from dying." Karpos batted a hand in the air as if swatting a fly then popped another fig in his mouth.

Amethea tucked a long, stray curl of her red hair back into her headband. Her hair had a mind of its own, full of untamed motion as if a scramble of squirrels lived in it. She worried her uncle might find it unseemly for he was a man, she had observed, who cared a great deal about appearances. She bowed her head, fighting an urge to argue with him. The future of her brother depended on her finding a way to soften her uncle's disdain.

Amethea longed to ask outright what his plans were for Hippasus but held her tongue. I must not appear impatient, she told herself, although concealing her emotions had never been easy. They could be as unruly and wild as her hair. And like her mother, Amethea was headstrong. Atalanta-strong she liked to think. What would Atalanta do now?

"My brother," she began.

But Karpos did not want to talk about Hippasus. Sunlight glittered on the hammered gold bands he wore on both wrists and his eyes roamed over her body once more. His gold bands made Amethea think of Hippomenes' golden apples, the bewitched apples that ended Atalanta's winning streak against the male runners of Greece. She felt suddenly wary. Karpos was after something, she sensed.

"What did your mother tell you about her victory at the Heraea Games?" he asked in a kinder voice. His eyes met hers and he smiled.

Why is he asking this, Amethea wondered. For as long as she could remember, Karpos had held nothing but contempt for her mother. Why was he now reminiscing about her mother's finest moment?

Karpos stroked the dark curls of his beard and peered at her as if trying to discern something in her expression. "Did she ever tell you about that day?" he asked again, grasping her wrist as she poured more wine. His arms were covered in thick, black hair. Like a bear, she thought, but not a loving bear like Atalanta's foster mother. His grasp tightened on her wrist

She cleared her throat. "Mother told me that she ran like the wind, that it was the happy day she met my father."

Karpos let go her wrist and leaned back, half gloating. He took another swig of wine and said, "Adelphos admired my sister's grace and speed. Your father was a famous athlete, you know. His name is still celebrated."

"Yes, Uncle. He won the pentathlon at Olympia. Three times in a row.'

"A woman is lucky to win one footrace," her uncle observed.

Amethea nodded and said, "Women do not race once they are married."

"Yes," her uncle agreed. "Only maidens are allowed to compete."

Karpos drained his cup and licked his lips. Something in the tone of his voice sent a quick rush of fear through Amethea's limbs. Had he already promised her to some unknown suitor?

She took a breath to steady herself and said, "Women run to honor the Mother Goddess. As my mother did."

"But a woman also honors her family and her city by winning. And a woman may have a victory statue made. Such a woman is a trophy to a husband when she weds."

An emotion other than grief or fear suddenly welled up in Amethea and it was bitter disappointment. Ever since she could remember, she had longed to compete in the women's footraces at Olympia, the Heraea Games, just as her mother had done. She longed to taste her own victory and have a statue made to stand alongside her mother's in Hera's Temple there. But her mother's death had made a once unlikely dream an impossible one. The Heraea Games, the most famous of all women's races, were held only once every four years to coincide with the men's Olympic Games. This year was the year, the only year she might have hoped to compete. Of course, the odds of her going had always been slim. Her mother had considered contacting Karpos to ask for his help but had quickly abandoned the idea, knowing how hostile he felt towards her.

"Your father saw the runner in you when you were born," Karpos said as he gave her another probing look. "Consider the name he gave you."

Amethea swallowed, straightened her shoulders and nodded, struggling to maintain her composure. Bitterly, she reflected that her name was the only thing she had left from her father. When she was born with a head of fiery red curls, Adelphos had named her after an immortal horse that pulls the sun god's chariot. She had lived up to the name, pulling herself up by her mother's knees at nine months to walk. As a toddler she chased butterflies on legs that lost their baby fat early.

"If your mother had been sensible, your own father would be accompanying you to the Heraea Games this summer," Karpos said.

Amethea knew her uncle was referring to her mother's refusal to have Hippasus exposed at birth. Yes, if her mother had relinquished Hippasus, allowed Adelphos to carry the baby up a mountainside and abandon him on a cold rock, life would be different. She would not have lost her father and there would be no question of her missing the Heraea Games. A faint but sour trace of resentment uncoiled in Amethea's heart like a hissing snake. She knew she was as gifted a runner as both her parents but she would never have a chance to prove it.

"Your mother's name is inscribed on a statue in Hera's Temple," Karpos continued. "It is a fine image. Such a pity you will never see it."

Did Karpos mention this to rub onion even deeper into her wound, Amethea wondered? She blinked back angry tears, hoping her uncle would not notice.

"Ah, but races are nothing to you now," he added. "You are in mourning, though I believe your mother wanted you to race at the Games more than she treasured her own pride."

Amethea jerked her head up in surprise and stared at Karpos. Had her mother contacted him, after all, and not told her about it?

"If circumstances had been different, I might have agreed to take you myself," he said. "But there are other things to attend to now." He popped a fig in his mouth and chewed it, spitting out a piece of the hard stem.

At that moment Dove bounded into the little courtyard and thrust her paws in Amethea's lap. She wagged her long, thin tail in a wide arc. Amethea looked up and saw Hippasus hesitating at the entrance to the garden.

Karpos stood up brusquely. "Men are required to give an oath that they have trained a full ten months before competing at the Olympics," he remarked. "No such requirement is laid upon girls, but those who are serious make themselves ready."

"I would have been ready, Uncle," Amethea said as she stroked Dove behind the ears.

"Indeed? An even greater pity then."

Before her mother fell ill, Amethea daily sprinted on narrow goat trails that wound through outcroppings of rock and rough pasture. Before sunset, she often ran along an empty stretch of beach, toughening her feet on pebbles and sand. A youth her age, named Eucles, sometimes ran along the same shore but they never spoke. She had heard he was training for the Olympic Games and knowing that had fueled her own stride.

"Will you stay for dinner, Uncle?" asked Amethea, anxious to change the subject. "We would be honored if you would share a simple meal with us." She opened her arm as if to invite her brother to step forward. He stood there with a bashful face, dangling a wild rabbit in one hand. His skill with a slingshot had brought home dinner. Stewed with wild greens, the rabbit would make a delicious meal. Yet she knew killing the rabbit had cost the gentle-hearted Hippasus. No doubt he did it to impress Karpos, to seek some small measure of approval.

But Karpos had already turned to depart. He bid farewell to Amethea and walked briskly past Hippasus without acknowledging he was there. Amethea stared after him feeling as if Karpos had slapped her in the face.

By the dim flickering of an olive oil lamp, Amethea entered her mother's chamber and undressed. She knelt by the garment chest and slowly lifted the wooden lid. On top were her mother's folded tunics and shawls woven from brightly dyed wool and linen. She pushed them aside to reveal a package wrapped in honey-colored goatskin. She unfolded the skin and slowly took out the chiton, a race garment, embroidered along the hem with images of dolphins and horses. She wrapped the knee-length rectangle of cloth around her body and fingered the fine stitches of her mother's handiwork. She blinked back tears. Even when it was hopeless, her mother had dared to believe Amethea might run at the Heraea Games. Amethea let the cloth drop to her feet, fell to her knees, and wept.

"Amethea, what is wrong?"

She turned and saw Hippasus leaning in the doorway of their mother's chamber. The flickering light from the lamp cast shadows on the wall that elongated the two bumps on his head into grotesque horns. She couldn't help giving a slight shudder. No wonder others found her brother hideous.

"It's nothing, Hippasus." she spoke harshly. "Go to sleep. It's late." Amethea hurriedly wrapped the chiton back in the goatskin, tossed it in the chest and slammed the lid down.

Later, she tossed on her sleeping couch, ashamed of her reaction to Hippasus. The shadows were to blame, she told herself. Her brother was not a satyr's son, no matter what Karpos and others may say. It was her duty to protect him, not win some fleeting glory in a race. Yet as she lay there in the dark, she could not entirely quell the realization that Hippasus did indeed bear the marks of a goat. What did the gods intend for him? for her?

The next morning, Karpos stopped by the cottage to inform Amethea that he was leaving by boat for Larisa but would return in a fortnight to escort her to his estate on the big island. She noticed he had trimmed his beard and his skin was scented with olive oil. He seemed unusually cheerful, as if a weight had been lifted from him.

"Pack your things," he instructed. "Although they are now freed from the terms of their service, I have asked Kimon and Dika to assist you in any way you need." He made no mention of Hippasus.

Amethea invited him to sit and offered him a treat Dika had prepared, sesame seeds mixed with honey and rolled into balls. She sat across from him as she had the day before and steadied herself with a deep breath. It couldn't wait any longer; she had to know what his plans were for Hippasus.

"Uncle," she began in a halting voice, "I know you were displeased with my mother—"

He interrupted. "My sister dishonored her husband by allowing the boy to live, and because of that your grandfather exiled her to Dia. But your mother has paid for her folly, and perhaps it is time I rest my own anger."

These were the last words Amethea expected to hear from Karpos and she looked up in astonishment.

"I once admired her, Amethea. She was such a fine runner! And I have been thinking, I cannot ignore the fact that I have a nephew. After all, every person may serve the gods."

Amethea blurted, "Then you accept Hippasus?" Her heart lifted for the first time in days.

Karpos' jaw briefly tensed. He half-closed his eyes and frowned. Amethea knew Hippasus filled her uncle with revulsion.

"Uncle, I promised my mother I would look after him. My brother is a good boy. I swear he will not be a burden."

Karpos surprised her further by taking her hands into his own as if to reassure her and said, "Of course, of course. I've had a great deal on my mind, and I'm sorry if you thought I had no plans for your brother. But you must trust me, I am making arrangements."

"Then you will not deny him; you will not abandon him?"

"The boy is ugly and slow as an ox in mind as well as limb. Do I speak harshly? I am only stating facts. But all may serve the gods, even a goat-footed boy."

Amethea sighed in relief. "Shall I pack his things, as well, then, for the move to Larisa?"

Karpos turned his face towards the white roses. A few new buds had appeared. "What? No, no, everything will be provided for. Best to leave his shepherd rags behind."

Karpos must intend, she suddenly realized, to provide Hippasus with the finery worthy of a nephew. Who would dare make fun of a goat-footed boy if he had the patronage of a wealthy, powerful man like Karpos? The cord of worry that had held her lungs in a suffocating grip since the night her mother died, loosened.

"Oh, Uncle, how can I show my gratitude?"

"Gratitude? No need, my niece. As I said, everything is being arranged. My daughters are looking forward to having a new sister."

Karpos wiped his mouth with the back of his hand and stood up. On his way out, he turned back and said. "There is one other thing, Amethea. Do not abandon your hope for a victory."

Amethea watched her uncle depart down the path towards the village, her skin tingling. She knew she shouldn't make too much of his parting words, but what if he meant he intended to take her to the Heraea Games, after all. Was it possible?

She quickly packed a meal, grabbed her aulos, and went to find Hippasus. She had warned him that Karpos would be visiting in the morning and had arranged to meet him later at the shrine. Sending him away from the cottage had been unnecessary, she now realized. She couldn't wait to tell him that Karpos intended to care for them both.

At the shrine that evening, Amethea played Hippasus' favorite tunes while he lined up pebbles and counted them. He arranged some of the pebbles into hexagons connected like the cells of a honeycomb. She paused and looked up at the stars until she located the lion and the pulsing blue star of his heart. There in the shrine of the Bee Goddess, she could almost see herself crossing the finish line at the Heraea Games.

CHAPTER FIVE

PASSING OUT
OF HADES

Melissa's spirits sank with every passing mile. Her father's face was grim. He'd hardly spoken a word as the solar van carried them across the sterile stretch of bleached desert called the Hell Zone. Thousands of abandoned fracking wells stood like nails in an enormous coffin, remnants of the last desperate push to extract fossil fuels. Whatever plants and animals had once lived here had either vanished or been forced north by the lack of water and a warming climate. Occasionally an eco-drone passed overhead, monitoring for any sign of life.

The landscape was so bleak, it was hard to imagine anything good could exist on the other side of it, but gradually as they drew nearer to Texas, they began to pass solar farms with rows of sleek rotating mirrors and after that, small towns centered around large plazas filled with blooming desert plants. Green corridors of cacti and succulents connected these towns.

Her father told her that a specific moth or native bee or bat or beetle pollinated every plant in the corridors and that these towns had been tasked with saving desert pollinators from extinction. Their partial success, though far from certain, gave him hope for honeybees. In West Texas, giant wind tulips, tall as skyscrapers, lined the horizon. These had replaced older versions of wind turbines, the kind with blades that had proved so lethal to birds and bats.

And then, as if to welcome Melissa and her father in larger than life style, their solar van came to a sudden halt to allow a migration of tens of thousands of tarantulas to cross the road. Each furry arachnid was as large as her fist. Melissa's mouth dropped open and the origami bee she'd been folding fell from her hands.

"We're still some hours from Benefit," her father said. "You'll be surprised how much greener the Hill Country is."

CHAPTER SIX

BEAU

Hermes sniffed the fence line that separated the neighbor's goat farm from the Bùi family's new yard. Melissa sat on a weathered cypress bench placed beneath the wide branches of a live oak tree. Morning sunlight, hot on her cheeks, filtered through gnarled and twisting branches. She rubbed her palms, beaded with sweat, on her shorts. The basket at her side was a third of the way filled with origami bees.

She'd promised to call Noi, her grandmother, once they were settled in Benefit and now seemed as good a time as any. They'd been in the college town for a week and because they had few belongings and the cottage was already half-furnished with simple furniture, it hadn't taken long to arrange things. The little house felt comfortable, even homey, although Melissa was not ready to accept it as home.

"Noi?" she tapped her holographic wristband and in seconds an image of her smiling grandmother rose into the air.

"I'm glad to see you!" her grandmother said in a chirpy voice, her black eyes sparkling. Her hair was pulled back in a bun secured with a red lacquered chopstick and Melissa could see her grandmother was sitting at her kitchen table with her cat. The slender Siamese was licking the last specks of rice porridge from a bowl the same blue as his eyes.

Mechtild Tran was a quilt artist who lived in San Francisco. She was holding a piece of cloth and a threaded needle. Her smile faded as she scrutinized her granddaughter's face.

"Something bothering you, little bee?"

Melissa hesitated, and then said, "I had a couple seizures right before the move."

Noi pursed her lips in a small frown. "Hmmm. Bad ones?"

"No, just a little different."

"How so?" Noi leaned slightly forward as if Melissa were about to share a secret.

Melissa lifted a finger to the bridge of her nose and rubbed it. "Well, I thought I heard music that no one else did."

"Hmm. But nothing else? No tremors?"

"No."

"What did your father say?"

"He said it was probably a pre-seizure aura and we'd keep an eye on it."

"That's sensible. You know, Melissa, I sometimes hear unusual sounds prior to seizures."

"I know, but I never have before."

"Well, I like to think of them as the voices of apsara." Noi giggled. Apsara, Melissa knew, were celestial nymphs in Buddhist fairy tales. Only Noi could think of seizures so poetically.

Her grandmother's voice lowered and in a more serious tone, she asked, "But these recent episodes of yours, you've just blanked out? No convulsions? Nothing else?"

"No."

An odd look that seemed a mixture of both relief and disappointment crossed Noi's face. Then she smiled and held her quilting needle up with its tail of silver thread. "So tell me about Benefit. Better yet, quilt me a square that shows it to me."

Melissa lifted her basket to show her grandmother. "Actually, I'm working on an origami project right now."

"Ah. Are those bees?"

Melissa explained her plan to fold one thousand honeybees and Noi clucked approval.

"A wonderful idea! Good to dedicate your efforts to bring the bees back."

Melissa shrugged doubtfully. "It's not like folding a bunch of paper bees will bring any real ones back, but I want to show Ba I support his efforts." She sifted a hand through the basket of bees.

"Never underestimate what imagination and mindful hands can accomplish." Noi made a few even stitches, small as sesame seeds, then pulled her needle through the cloth in her hand.

Noi was an artist through and through. Melissa wished she had Noi's faith that the world of honeybees could be restored. The truth was, Melissa wasn't at all sure that any of her own actions could make a difference in the wrecked world she'd been born into. So many species gone, so many layers of life faded.

"Don't tell Ba, okay? I want it to be a surprise."

Noi nodded and looked up from her quilting, startling Melissa with a sharp, probing look. "I will be as silent as a stone.

Fold each bee with faith, nhé!" Noi's last word, Vietnamese for something akin to 'okay?' reminded Melissa of the sound of a small bell.

"I will, Noi. I miss you!"

"I miss you, too. It's a good thing we have our holograms. Call me if you have another seizure." Mechtild Tran was no stranger to seizures because she herself was epileptic.

"Okay, Noi. Talk to you soon."

Melissa hesitated before picking up another piece of origami paper. She wasn't sure she wanted to tell anyone, not even Noi, about her seizures. She wasn't supposed to have them anymore. The doctor said most kids grew out of them. She hated being defective, hated the way kids giggled or pointed at her when she came out of a seizure in the middle of class. And the way some kids called her "statue girl." Maybe Noi had made peace with being an epileptic, but Melissa couldn't.

I want a life that is whole, she thought, not one with holes cut out of it. She tried to shift her focus. Noi wanted her to quilt a square of the Texas Hill Country. How would that look? Patches of dull olive for live oak trees. Chalk color for limestone canyons. Pale gray for cypress that grew along the Sabinal. The sluggish river, of course, would be a patch of brown and green. Threads of mauve and purple for the lavender field where the Yolo bees now lived, where her father and his team were trying to keep the last of North America's honeybees alive. In her mind, Melissa rehearsed embroidery stitches, but the thing was, she didn't really want to stitch her new landscape. The place she didn't want to be.

She wiped her sweaty palms on her shorts and completed the base folds for another bee. It was so muggy, it was hard to get the damp paper to hold a sharp crease. She bent over to get a tricky crimp fold right and swatted unsuccessfully at a mosquito that landed on her hand.

Her father told her that Benefit had once been a lush center of lavender production with meadows stretching in all directions. There were fewer lavender fields now. Fewer trees. Thousands of majestic oaks had toppled during long years of thirst, as had centuries-old cypress trees whose roots depended on the river. The past couple of years had seen somewhat better rainfall and the Sabinal, though sluggish and shallow, was flowing again. But who knew how long that would last?

Melissa tugged at two corners of her origami bee to pull the wings into position, and once again, wondered, why Texas, why here? Mom is so much luckier, she thought, living on an island in the crystal blue waters of the Aegean Sea.

She placed the finished bee in the basket and couldn't help feeling a small swell of pride. She was good with her hands. An ability, Noi had assured her, passed down through a long line of Vietnamese grandmothers. Her lips turned up in a half smile as she remembered how Noi had scooped her hands into her own when Melissa was only four years old and closely examined the fingerprint whorls on each of Melissa's finger pads. She had clucked in approval.

"Eight complete whorls. That means you have talent for fine work. For careful detail." Noi had proceeded, on the spot, to teach Melissa how to sew a straight line on a piece of muslin.

Melissa was glad to have inherited skillful hands from her grandmother. Unfortunately, she had also inherited the blank-out form of epilepsy. Noi had been known to go blank for several minutes at a time, several times a day. How can she stand it, Melissa wondered, because her grandmother always seemed so solid and cheerful?

Melissa stood up from the bench and stretched her arms over her head. She ambled back into the house and poured herself a tall glass of ice water, then sat on the porch swing, swaying slowly back and forth. At least Ba wasn't making her start school right away. She had managed to take her final exams back in California early, and after several arguments, her father had finally agreed to wait until the fall to enroll her at Benefit Middle School. She was not looking forward to it. Teachers would have to be informed about her seizures. Kids would find her blank-outs weird.

Well, at least for now, she could stay at home, fold her origami, and look up holo-vids. Some days her father didn't return until well past dark. That night, alone in the house, she lay beneath the whir of a ceiling fan in her room and listened to the distant yips of a coyote. Hermes curled his body against hers. As she drifted off to sleep, the faint lilt of a flute mingled with the coyote's ghostly cries.

The next morning, Melissa sat at her same spot on the cypress bench and began another round of origami. Hermes again explored scents along the fence line as she folded her gold and black squares of paper into bees. Goats foraged in the meadow on the other side of the fence. Melissa had not yet met the neighbors and had forgotten about the thirteen-year-old boy who lived there.

She was working on a complex wing fold when she heard the flute, muted at first but soon clear and insistent. Her arms tingled and she felt a rush of fear. She jerked upright in an unsuccessful attempt to ward off the seizure, but the meadow with its goats dissolved. Everything vanished save for the haunted trills of the flute. Then there was a flash of light and she was looking at a different meadow. She saw a teenage girl, the one she had seen before, place a pair of flutes on a rock where a young boy with curly brown hair and pale eyes sat. There was something odd about the boy. His right foot ended in a knob that looked almost like a hoof and two horn-like bumps protruded from his brow. A slender hound lay beside him and he held a small goat, a kid, in his lap. He clapped his hands as the girl took her place behind a line scratched in the dirt. She crouched down, lifted her hips, and then burst into a sprint to the other side of the meadow. With a joyous whoop, the boy threw his arms into the air. The startled kid leapt from his lap and butted its head against him in protest.

Then something pushed against Melissa's own back and she twirled around to see a small goat with curly strands of chocolate colored fleece. She was back on the cypress bench, her basket of bees beside her, a completed bee in her hand. She glanced from goat to bee and back to goat. What had just happened, another hallucination?

The goat's narrow face and dainty hooves were black, but its eyes were a startling sapphire blue. Hermes trotted back to Melissa's side protectively and deciding the goat was not a threat, turned his head to ignore it.

Half-dazed, Melissa reached towards the goat and ran her fingers through its soft fleece to convince herself it was real. The goat nuzzled its head against her thigh. It was real all right, but Melissa felt strangely drained as if part of her was still in that other meadow. Her arms felt light as air as if she'd somehow lost substance. She'd had another hallucination, seen the girl and boy again. And in her hand rested a perfect origami bee. She hadn't folded those wings yet, had she? She felt a sudden wave of nausea.

At that moment a boy about her age ran into the yard and stopped just short of the bench. He was tall and slight with olive skin and wavy chestnut hair, dressed in a pair of cut-offs and t-shirt. The look on his face was a mixture of relief and exasperation.

"Found you, Amaltheia!" He held a collar attached to a leash, which he placed around the goat's neck as if she were a dog. He turned to Melissa. "Sorry. Amaltheia picks locks on goat-proof gates. I guess she wanted to check out our new neighbors."

Melissa just stared at him. Barely recovered from her hallucination, the boy's sudden appearance felt like an invasion.

"Amaltheia, she's harmless. You're not afraid of goats, are you?"

What a ridiculous question. Melissa shook her head. "Of course not."

The boy looked hard at her then at the origami bee in her hands.

"Are you okay? You look like you just saw a ghost."

Just go away, she wanted to say, but she managed a curt, "I'm fine."

He reached out a finger and touched the origami bee.

"Did you fold that?"

"No, my dog did."

"Talented dog. Maybe he could teach my goat." The boy laughed.

Melissa dropped the bee into the basket and shoved the basket under the bench. She felt embarrassed. What if the boy had seen her in her blank-out state? She wished he'd take the goat and leave.

Without warning, the blue-eyed goat thrust its head under the bench and grabbed a large mouthful of bees. Chomp.

"Hey, that's not food!" scolded Melissa as she snatched the basket.

"Dang!" The boy jerked the goat back and pulled a bee from its mouth. He wiped it on his cutoffs and handed it back to Melissa. "Still intact, just a little chewed."

Melissa made a face, took the bee and dropped it back in the basket.

"Look, I'm double sorry. Amaltheia will taste just about anything to see if it's worth eating."

The goat spit out a few bees, chewed beyond repair, then gave a little bleat. She was cute Melissa had to admit. Those startling blue eyes, the strands of curly chocolate fleece. But she'd probably devoured a half-day's worth of folding.

"Her name is Amaltheia?" Despite wanting the boy to disappear, Melissa was curious about the goat's name. Thanks to her mother, she knew her Greek mythology.

"Yeah, named after the goat that suckled Zeus." He gave her another hard look. "You sure you're okay? You look kind of queasy."

"I'm fine. Really."

"So how come you're folding all those bees?"

The boy was nosy. "Just something I'm working on."

"How come I haven't seen you in school?"

Impossibly nosy. "My dad said I could wait to enroll in the fall."

"Wow, you're lucky."

"How come you're not in school? Isn't today a school day?"

"Suspended for the day. And tomorrow, too. Sometimes, I have to make my own luck." He smiled, obviously pleased with himself.

Nosy and bad news. Melissa really wanted him to leave.

"You're wondering who the hell I am, right?"

Melissa didn't answer.

"My name is Beau, I live next door." He extended a hand that Melissa now noticed was covered in a layer of cracked, red clay.

He wiped his hand on his cut-offs. "It's just clay."

She reluctantly shook his hand. "I'm Melissa."

"Yeah, I know. Well, I need to take Amaltheia back. See you around."

Hopefully not anytime soon, thought Melissa, as she watched Beau lead Amaltheia out the gate. She picked up her basket of bees and went inside the house to wash the clay off her hand and then lay down. She still felt queasy. The boy hadn't said anything about seeing her blanked out, but had he? Should she call Noi and tell her about the seizure? Should she tell her father? She didn't want to admit something strange was happening to her. She didn't want to go back on meds and she knew that would be her father's first and only response.

At sunset, Melissa sat on the porch swing swaying back and forth, still debating whether or not to tell her father about her seizure. She had decided against calling Noi. What could her grandmother, two thousand miles away, do anyway? Finally, she got up and went to the kitchen to boil rice noodles for dinner. She stir-fried some tofu and chopped a handful of fresh herbs. Their peppery, lemony scent helped ease the nausea she'd felt all day. She and her father had traveled from California with potted herbs that were now lined up along the porch. No meal, her father insisted, was complete without a generous sprinkling of fresh herbs like violet basil, coriander leaf or what everyone called cilantro in Texas, and mint. Some herbs could be hand-pollinated in the absence of bees, a tricky and time-consuming task, but worth it to break the bland monotony of vegetable and fruit deprived meals. Fruity and Veggie Pills, in their bright and chewable shapes, were no substitute for the real thing. Of course, in many cases, Melissa didn't even know what the real thing tasted like.

The sky, drained of the day's fierce light, darkened at the kitchen window. Melissa turned on a small lamp and waited for the water to boil. The cooked noodles sat in a colander, clumped and cold, before she heard the sound of her father's bike glide over the driveway gravel. He entered the kitchen with a long face. He nodded at Melissa and sat at the table she had set with bowls and chopsticks. He didn't even say hello.

"Ready for dinner, Ba?"

"I'm not that hungry." He stood up to wash his hands at the kitchen sink and sat back down. The lamplight cast shadows across his face and darkened the circles under his eyes.

They held their palms together, like lotus buds Noi would say, and softly intoned a Buddhist prayer, "Countless beings have cooperated to bring us this meal. May we use this nourishment for the good of all beings."

Her father picked up his pair of chopsticks and halfheartedly lifted a mouthful of noodles.

"You okay, Ba?"

"Bees went missing today."

"Missing?"

"Our Yolo bees, the ones we stole."

"You mean rescued?" Melissa wished her father would look up at her but he just stared into his noodles.

"Tried to rescue." Her father's voice was tinged with fatigue, disappointment.

"What do you mean?"

"When I checked on the hive, there must have been a quarter of them gone."

"Couldn't they have been out in the fields?" asked Melissa.

"Bees return to their hive before dark. These didn't." Her father frowned and put his chopsticks down.

The kitchen seemed suddenly drained of light as if each lost Yolo bee had been a candle blown out by an uncaring wind. Since the night of the bee heist, Melissa had thought of the bees as a bridge to her father, at least one shared experience that bonded them, even if Ba didn't feel that way. But he'd just called them "our Yolo bees," so maybe he did.

"They may have been sick when we found them." Her father grew silent and Melissa couldn't think of anything to say to cheer him up. She considered showing him all the origami bees she'd been folding, but decided against it. She was a long way from a thousand, and they were only paper bees.

Her father left half a bowl of noodles uneaten and got up from the table. "I need to finish up some lab notes and think about ways to avoid losing the rest of the colony. Bella and I are working on some things."

"Bella?"

"She's the mathematician on our team and has some new ideas about how honeybees communicate. She lives next door, you know."

"Oh yeah, I'd forgotten."

Melissa washed the dishes then half-heartedly tossed a Frisbee by porch light to Hermes in the back yard. He was the opposite of half-hearted, a canine athlete who excelled at spirited dashes, leaps, and mid-air twists. He rarely missed a catch so when he failed to go after a throw and instead stood with ears cocked and an expectant look on his face, followed by a warning bark, Melissa knew that they had visitors. Sure enough, Beau and two women appeared at the gate. Melissa wanted to vanish but they had already seen her and one of the women walked right up to her and extended a hand. It was easy to tell she must be Beau's biological mother because although she was short and slightly plump, she had the same wavy chestnut hair and a crinkle at the corner of her green eyes, like Beau, when she smiled. The other woman was tall and angular with skin the hue of a cocoa bean. Her salt and pepper hair was tightly curled and short-cropped, her eyes a warm shade of amber brown like a cup of jasmine tea.

"Mucho gusto. It's Melissa, right? Beau enjoyed meeting you today and so did Amaltheia. She's already trying to figure out the new lock I put on the gate." The woman with green eyes laughed then added, "I'm Rocio Valenzuela and this is Bella Garnet, a colleague of your father's. Please call us by our first names."

Melissa shook both women's hands but avoided looking at Beau who stood slightly behind the two women, a ball of clay in his hand and a drawstring cloth bag slung over one shoulder.

"Amaltheia's adorable," Melissa said, politely neglecting to add that the petite goat had devoured several hours of work.

"Goats are wonderful animals to work with," said Rocio. "Curious and playful, if a bit headstrong, but I like that. You should come by and meet the rest of them. Anytime you like."

"Thanks."

Bella gave a quick laugh. "Beau has done an admirable job of naming our goats after gods and goddesses. We have a veritable Mt. Olympus next door."

Melissa's father, hearing their voices, stepped out on the porch. "Bella! and this must be Rocio and Beau. Welcome! Come on up!"

Once on the porch, Beau handed Rocio the cloth bag he'd been carrying. She opened it and pulled out two jars of feta cheese, small white cubes packed with slices of sundried tomato. She handed them to Melissa's father.

"We make this to sell at the local farmers market, but we also share them at Benefit's weekly food swap on the library grounds. Do you know about the food swap? "

"No, but I'd like to."

"Looks like you've got herbs growing on your porch. Hand-pollinated? Herbs are great for swapping."

Beau raised an eyebrow and said, "Mom," in a slightly dis-approving voice.

Rocio Valenzuela caught herself and laughed. She had a rich, layered laugh, full of bell tones. She tapped Beau on the arm and said, "But I'm not proposing a swap right now. These jars of feta are a welcome gift."

Melissa's father thanked her, adding, "It's a real treat to have cheese."

Cheese and yogurt were infrequent items at the Bùi's din-ner table. And forget ice cream. No one could afford that luxury anymore. Dairy cows needed alfalfa and clover, both pollinated by bees.

"Our goats eat plants that cows do not," Rocio said, "and they're gentler on land and climate."

"Bella told me you run your household energy on biogas from goat manure. That's impressive," said Melissa's father.

"I've never tasted goat cheese," said Melissa, looking at the jars a little doubtfully.

"Pobrecita!" exclaimed Rocio. "I can see I need to take you under my wing."

Melissa was not anxious to be taken under a stranger's wing and when Rocio gave her a sudden hug, she felt embarrassed. But the spontaneous warmth of the hug touched something else. Her mother hugged like that. Her father never did. Melissa, her feelings all a-tangle, turned from Rocio towards the porch steps and wondered if she could make an escape.

But escape wasn't possible. Her father suggested they all sit on the covered porch. Sea breezes that travelled all the way from the Gulf of Mexico quickened the evening air and brought a welcome change from the day's oppressive heat. Melissa sat away from the group on the porch swing, and was annoyed when Beau came and sat on the other end. Hermes leapt up and sandwiched himself between them. The adults sat on mesquite rockers gathered round a table.

"Melissa, how about getting everyone something to drink? There's a pitcher of lemongrass tea in the fridge."

Beau followed Melissa into the kitchen—did he have to hover?—and helped her carry out trays with tumblers filled with ice and a plump, recycled glass pitcher.

Once everyone had been served, Rocio turned to Melissa and said, "Do you hand spin, Melissa? I know a lot of young people have taken up the old crafts."

"My Mom was going to show me," Melissa answered. "She has some spindles, but she never had time, so—"

"Oh, I'd be happy to show you! Beau says you're not in school and it must get boring staying home alone. Come over tomorrow and I'll give you a first lesson."

"Well, I might have to do some stuff," Melissa began.

"I think that's a great idea," interrupted her father.

Melissa gave her father a pleading look but his head was already bent over a foldable tablet that Bella had taken from her pocket.

"Then it's settled," said Rocio. "Come first thing in the morning before it gets too hot. I'll show you how to spin pygora fibers. They're very soft."

"Pygora?" asked Melissa.

"Pygora," Beau repeated. He was kneading a ball of clay in his hands and did not look up while he spoke. "Amaltheia's a pygora, a cross between an angora and a pygmy. She gets her blue eyes from the angora side."

Well, he knew his goats, but what was with that ball of red clay? Were his hands always covered in red dirt? And why had he been suspended?

"Mom," Beau said, "if you saw Melissa's origami, you know she'd be good at spinning."

Surprised by the unexpected compliment, Melissa could almost hear her grandmother clucking, "Eight whorls!"

Her father spoke in a quiet voice to Bella. "What's this here? Any luck with that quark equation?"

Bella nodded. "I'm close, Paul. Close."

"Quarks?" Beau looked up from his clay.

"Sorry, a little bit of shop talk," said Melissa's father.

"Mind explaining?" asked Beau. "We just learned about quarks in science."

Melissa glanced at Beau. She hadn't taken him for the academic type.

"Do quarks have something to do with bees?" Beau persisted.

"I don't want to bore anyone," said Bella.

"You are never boring, Bella," Rocio said.

"You are too kind," she responded, then took a sip of iced tea before turning to Melissa and Beau.

"I'm sure you know," she began, "that honeybees perform dances to show other bees where to find nectar sources." The mathematician moved her hands lightly through the air in figure eights as if to mimic the bees' dancing. "We know a lot about how the dances work and have for over a century, but there's still a lot we can't explain."

"And that's where quarks might come in," said Melissa's father.

"Turns out," continued Bella, "that a honeybee dance can be mapped using a six-dimensional pattern in mathematics."

"Hold on," said Beau. "Are you saying a honeybee dances in six dimensions?"

Melissa noticed the clump of clay in his hands was assuming some kind of animal shape. She also noticed that Hermes had rested his head on Beau's leg. Disloyal dog.

"Not that exactly," said Bella, "but I believe they might be able to detect and pass on information that is tucked in higher dimensions. You see, quarks are mapped using the exact same pattern."

"Wait a minute," said Melissa, "what are quarks?"

"You know what atoms are?" Beau looked at her.

"Of course." Did Beau think she was a complete moron? Maybe he really had seen her blank out earlier and decided she had a damaged brain. Uneasy, she shifted her position on the porch swing.

"And neutrons and protons, right?"

"Yes."

"Well, quarks are even smaller. They make up neutrons and protons."

"Oh." Melissa said, feeling stupid. She was a whiz at math, but had she missed that information in science class? She remembered getting in trouble a few times after getting caught folding origami during science. Or maybe the teacher had mentioned quarks when she was in seizure mode. Statue girl might have missed any number of details.

"So you're saying bee dances and quarks share some kind of multi-dimensional connection?" Beau cocked his head towards Bella, his hands still working his ball of clay.

"It's still in the hypothesis stage, Beau, but I believe honeybees might exchange tiny holographic maps, maps made of quarks coiled in higher dimensions that they share during their wiggle and waggle dances."

"That would be amazing," Beau said. "Quarks are cool. Mr. Alvarez said they blink in and out of existence in some kind of weird motion that makes matter possible."

Melissa stared at Beau. It was hard to imagine the same boy getting suspended. He held up his ball of clay and smashed it into a formless glob, then went back to modeling something new.

"That's right," said Bella. "Quarks along with sticky particles called gluons are what make matter *matter*. They make things cohere, make things seem solid to us."

"Gluons, like glue?" Melissa asked. She felt almost dizzy at the thought of tiny particles popping in and out of existence, blinking on and off.

"That's right," said Bella. "Inside every atom there's a mysterious soup of quarks and sticky gluons holding matter together. If honeybees can sense those patterns, it might help them make sophisticated nectar maps and at phenomenal speeds."

Rocio shook her head. "I pride myself on being able to communicate with goats. But this quark stuff, it's way beyond me."

Bella shook her head. "I have an equally hard time understanding goat speak."

"Maaa, maaa!" responded Rocio. They all laughed.

"Will your research help bring the bees back?" Melissa asked.

Her father cleared his throat. "We think the long use of pesticides and stressors like parasites and climate change may have damaged honeybee abilities to use their multi-dimensional communication system. If we can figure out how it worked, we might have a shot at restoring and healing that system in their brains." He stood up and stretched, then ambled into the house. When he came back out, he had two pairs of scissors in his hands and invited Beau's mothers to clip any herbs they wanted from the pots lining the porch.

While his mothers gathered herbs, Beau's foot kept the porch swing gently swaying back and forth. Melissa hadn't noticed when Beau put up his modeling clay, but his hands were empty now and he was rubbing them on his cut-offs. Laundry must be a constant chore at his house.

Beau's mothers were soon thanking her father for a pleasant evening. Beau stood up, muttered, "Hasta luego," then followed the two women down the porch steps and out the gate.

Balancing several tumblers in her hands, Melissa watched their guests depart. A plump gibbous moon shone and the night pulsed with the thrum of crickets. She looked up in the sky to locate Regulus, the lion's heart. Then as she turned back towards the kitchen, she noticed a small figurine on the porch table. She set the glasses down to take a closer look. There sat a perfect little rendition of Hermes in red clay.

CHAPTER SEVEN

MOUNT OLYMPUS

Melissa ate a bowl of rice, washed the bowl, and brushed her teeth. In slow motion. She did not want to walk next door for a spinning lesson. Why had her father insisted she go? If he was so concerned about her spending too much time alone, why didn't he spend more time at home himself? What if she had a seizure when she was at Beau's house? Finally, unable to delay any longer, she tucked a package of origami paper and a water bottle in her shoulder bag and trudged next door. Not that she planned to do any folding while she was there, it's just she never went anywhere without origami paper. Maybe it was a bit like Beau and his clay.

Rocio met her at the door, all smiles and warmth. "I'm glad you're here, Melissa! I've tried to teach Beau to spin because he has talent in his hands but all he wants to do is clay, always his clay."

Rocio led Melissa into a room where the walls were lined with shelves stuffed with skeins of hand-dyed yarns. A spinning wheel sat in one corner and a large loom took up half of the room. There were fibers soaking in tubs and willow baskets that held drop spindles, wool carders, and knitting needles. A hand-loomed rug covered most of the red tile floor. The rich colors and textures reminded Melissa of her grandmother's quilting studio and she felt a sudden pang of homesickness.

It was tricky at first to wrap pygora fibers around a spindle and let the spindle drop and twirl to twist the fibers into yarn. But under Rocio's patient guidance, Melissa soon found herself able to keep a steady rhythm going. Drop, rotate, pinch the strand and pull. Drop, rotate, pinch and pull. She learned to wind the lengthening strand of spun yarn beneath the whorl that was located at the top end of the spindle's smooth shaft. The whorl on Melissa's spindle was shaped like a spinning top and made of clay. The repetitive nature of spinning was almost like the repetitive strides of running and Melissa found it soothing. Drop, rotate, pinch and pull.

"Hey, Mom," the sound of Beau's voice as he entered the room with an armful of fibers startled Melissa and she dropped her spindle. It fell with a dull thud on the rug and rolled towards Beau. He dumped the mohair fibers, cream and tan colored, into a wooden bin then stooped over to pick up the spindle. He handed it back to an embarrassed Melissa with an unceremoni-ous "Hi, Mel," then turned back to his mother, "That's it until the winter sheering. Pandora was the last goat that had anything left to hand-pluck."

"That's my spindle you're using," he said to Melissa.

"Oh, I thought your Mom said you didn't spin."

"I don't. I made the spindle whorl."

Melissa took a closer look at the whorl made of fired white clay. It was painted with a design of red and black zigzag-ging lines.

"I got the design from a Greek vase."

"Huh. My Mom would like it."

"Did you repair the back fence?" interrupted Rocio.

"Yes, and swept out all the sheds."

"And shoveled manure for the biogas generator?"

"Yes, Mom."

He turned back to Melissa and shrugged. "Extra chores for getting suspended."

"Ai," sighed Rocio. "let it be the last time this year, por favor."

"It will be."

"Tired of spinning?" he asked Melissa. "Want to meet the rest of the goats?"

"Um, I'm not sure the lesson is over—"

"No, no, that's plenty for today," said Rocio. "Go meet the goats!"

"Bring any origami paper?" asked Beau as they walked out the back door towards the meadow.

"Well, there's some in my bag."

"Bring it along. I want to learn how to fold one of those bees."

"It's a lot of steps." And I'm not sure I want to show you, thought Melissa, then felt a tad guilty. After all she'd been using his spindle. And he'd left that perfect little clay figure of Hermes the night before.

"Don't you want to show me?"

She went back for her shoulder bag.

As they stood in the meadow, Beau pointed out the goats one by one. "For the goats, I chose minor deities over the big twelve, more interesting, I think." Amaltheia came leaping towards them and Melissa rubbed her hands through the goat's soft fleece. Beau introduced her to Echo and Asclepius, Orpheus and Pandora, Eos and Iris.

"Come with me. You haven't met Hera and Athena yet."

"I thought you said you didn't name any goats after the big twelve."

"Oh, these aren't goats."

Beau led her to one side of the meadow and introduced her to two llamas, one snowy white, the other a deep mahogany brown. They scrutinized Melissa with large, languid eyes then turned back to browsing.

"Let me guess. Llama cheese?"

"Nah, they're guard dogs. No coyote ever gets past Hera and Athena."

The teens sat down in the shade of an oak tree and Melissa took a swig of her water. "You seem to like Greek stuff."

"I devoured holo-comics about Greek myths as a little kid, but it's their sculpture I find interesting now. That's why I've been suspended three times this year."

"For liking sculpture?"

"No, for modeling with clay when I should be taking notes or answering test questions. I tend to blow off stuff I find boring. Some teachers take it personally."

Even now, Melissa noticed, he'd pulled out his ball of red clay and was molding it as they sat there.

"You're always fiddling with that ball of clay." Of course, she often had a piece of origami paper in her hands. Would the teachers here suspend her, too, she wondered?

"It's practice. Like practicing the piano, building muscle memory in my fingers. I want to capture the essence of people and animals. Like you do with origami."

"I don't know. Origami's more like engineering than art."

"But your bees, they have true bee-ness. That's what I like about them."

"They're just paper." She paused then added, "I liked the little Hermes." Beau, she realized, had perfectly captured Hermes-ness in red clay.

"Thanks." He picked a long spear of grass and nibbled the end. "You said your Mom would like the whorl, why?"

"She's an archeologist."

"Cool. Do you ever get to go on digs with her?"

"Sometimes, but she's in Crete right now, on a little island called Dia."

"Divorced?"

"What do you mean?"

"Your parents, they're divorced, right?"

Melissa didn't know what business it was of Beau's. "Yeah, but it's no big deal."

They sat without speaking for a minute and then Beau said, "So how come you're folding so many bees?"

"No reason really."

"Okay, don't tell me, but I know there's got to be a reason."

Melissa stood up. "I really should be going home. I left Hermes in the house."

"You won't show me how to fold a bee then?"

Melissa hesitated. "I really do need to let Hermes outside."

"That's okay. I'll come over with you and then you can show me."

He was obstinate, this Beau. Couldn't he take a hint?

She sighed, and said, "Fine, if you really want, come over and I'll show you how to fold one. But I warn you, it's a lot of steps." She stood up and turned to go.

"I may surprise you." Beau tossed the spear of grass and joined her.

As they sat on the cypress bench, Hermes napping beneath it, Melissa showed Beau the folds and had him practice on larger squares of paper until he got the hang of it. He had a quick memory and his folds were sharp and neat. Melissa noticed he had nice hands, brown and long-fingered with wide palms.

They folded without saying much. Sunlight glinted through the oak tree's brittle leaves and Melissa looked up to see two turkey vultures trading rings of flight in the sky. Halfway through folding a bee, she rested her hands for a moment to watch their graceful flight. They swooped low enough for her to see the white tips of their black wings before they soared high in the sky again.

Without warning, a sudden chill raced down her arms to her fingertips and the faint sound of a flute reached her ears. She stiffened but didn't take her eyes off the vultures and again they dipped low enough for her to see their white heads and golden brown wings. Wait. Hadn't their wings been black, tipped with white, just a moment before? She blinked and when she opened her eyes again found she was standing near the edge of a low cliff overlooking a sparkling turquoise sea. She turned her head slightly and saw a boy sitting on a large flat stone staring blankly ahead.

He had been attaching strings to a lyre balanced on his lap. His legs were crossed, but she could see he had a deformed foot that looked like a hoof. It was the same boy she'd seen before. In the distance someone else, the girl no doubt, was playing the flute, the same song that mingled with coyote cries when Melissa drifted to sleep. As she stared at the boy, the sound of the flute faded, replaced by the rattling drone of cicadas. A quick tremor passed through the boy's body and he looked down at his palm with an expression of surprise. He looked up and his eyes met Melissa's. At first his eyes widened in terror but then he bowed his head and raised his hands. What was he holding? It looked like, but no, it couldn't be. He closed his hand in a soft fist and lifted it to his ear, his face filled with wonder. Then he faded from sight.

"Mel, are you alright? Melissa!"

Melissa startled as Beau's face came into focus. His eyes searched hers and he clutched her arm in a firm, concerned grasp. She shook his hand off, realizing with horror that she had had a seizure. This was no brief staring spell; she had traveled again to that place by the sea. There had been the haunting sound of the flute, the same odd boy. This time, the boy held something in his hand. Melissa looked down at her own empty ones.

"Are you sick or something? You turned so pale I thought you were going to faint."

Melissa tried to collect herself. "I'm not used to the heat, that's all."

"Mel, you were staring in space like you couldn't see or hear me."

This was what she dreaded, having a seizure in front of other kids, and then forever after being thought weird or damaged. She wanted to run into the house, slam the door, and never see Beau again, but she turned to him and steadied herself with a deep breath.

"I have epilepsy. I get seizures where I blank out." There, she'd said it.

"Are you going to have convulsions?" Beau looked worried.

"No, it's not like that. I don't have that kind of epilepsy, I just…" Her voice faltered as she blinked back tears. She turned to look at the meadow.

Beau touched her arm lightly as if to reassure her and asked, "Can I do anything to help? Do you need to lie down?"

"I'm okay." She lifted a finger and rubbed the small bump at the bridge of her nose, that place where her Asian and Scottish ancestry met to make her nose neither Asian nor Celtic. Why, oh why, did she have to have a seizure in front of Beau? Now he would know she was a girl with holes in her mind. He was so darn nosy and talkative, he would tell everyone else. Soon the whole town would know.

"Should I call your father?"

"What? No. Ba doesn't need to know."

"Ba?"

"Ba is Vietnamese for Dad. It's what I call him."

"Like baa, baa black sheep, have you any wool?"

Melissa grimaced.

"Sorry, stupid joke."

Melissa smiled weakly. "I don't need to bother him. He's got enough on his mind."

"Look, I know he's trying to save civilization and all, but he's your father. Shouldn't we call him?"

"No. Really. It's not a big deal."

"You get these spells often?"

"No, hardly ever."

Beau gave her a dubious look. "I can call your Dad."

"No," Melissa said more forcefully. "Look, I think I'll go inside and read a book or something."

Beau's green eyes searched her own. "Okay. Thanks for showing me how to fold an origami bee."

"You must have whorls on your fingertips."

"Excuse me?"

"Nothing, it just means you're good at it."

"You're an odd fish, Mel. Well, if you're sure you're okay, I need to get back home and finish my chores."

Beau stood up and without looking back, leapt over the low fence and jogged across the meadow. Melissa didn't expect she'd see him again any time soon. What boy wanted to hang out with a girl who had staring spells?

The rest of the afternoon she lay on her bed, Hermes curled against her. She had that scary, weird feeling again that something inside her had been drained or erased. She didn't know which was worse, to lose parcels of time or hallucinate things that weren't really there. Why did she keep seeing that goat-like boy? And why on earth had he been holding an origami bee?

CHAPTER EIGHT

THE BEE MAKER

On her way to meet her brother, Amethea passed Kimon sitting in the shade of a wild chestnut tree. He nodded respectfully then returned to whittling a piece of wood. He was making a new flute to sell at market alongside Dika's baskets of sesame seeds. His father, Amethea knew, had been a sculptor, a trade Kimon would have followed if he hadn't been captured in a raid and sold as a slave. He'd offered to carve a marble stele for her mother's grave but Karpos had dismissed the idea. She also knew Kimon longed to work again with marble and bronze as much as she longed to run. If circumstances were different, she might have asked him to carve her victory statue. Her shoulders tensed and she frowned. Despite efforts to banish thoughts of the Heraea Games, they continued to rise with a power of their own. Why should she, after all, abandon the talent that was hers? Hadn't Karpos hinted he might be willing to take her to the Games? Or had she imagined that's what he meant?

The goats were scattered nearby like a handful of tossed knucklebones. Some rested beneath squat pine trees; others had climbed to sit on low branches to chew their cuds. A stalwart patriarch of the flock with curved horns that swept back from his head, browsed the rocky meadow for thistles and sea squill. Here and there, wild thyme and rosemary grew in thick tufts and pink peonies and spiny acanthus poked through the rocky soil. The hum of honeybees made a drowsy music.

Hippasus was in his usual spot on a flat white stone close to the shrine, a half-strung lyre in his lap. He appeared to have stopped in the middle of attaching and tightening strings and was staring straight ahead, unaware of Amethea's arrival. This, too, was not unusual. Hippasus frequently had spells, moments during which he seemed to travel far away. Dika liked to claim he was communing with Pan for she believed that his goat foot and head bumps were a sign of patronage from the shepherd god she revered. To her, an association with Pan was nothing to be ashamed of. Hippasus, for his part, never spoke about what he saw or heard during his spells. Sometimes after an episode, he drew shapes in the dirt, lined up sticks, or arranged pebbles in patterns.

Amethea did not disturb Hippasus but took a hard look at him, at his hoof-like foot and the bumps that resembled small horns on his head. She couldn't deny it. He was goat-like. Had her mother been right to save him at birth? She felt her cheeks flush with shame. How could she think such a thought?

But conversations with Karpos had led Amethea to think more about her father than she had in years. If Hippasus had been exposed at birth as her father wanted, a proud Adelphos would this very summer be accompanying Amethea to the Heraea Games. Why had the gods granted her swift legs if she could never prove them in a race?

Hippasus sat with his good leg tucked beneath him and his goat-foot stretched out before him. It was how the goats preferred to rest, one leg tucked under, one leg stretched out. His misshapen foot was a hindrance that hobbled his walking and he could not run at all—though he could scramble up and down the low coastal cliffs of their island home nearly as well as the goats. Even his coloring was goat-like. His skin was light brown and his chin-length hair was the same color as the dark brown band around the kri-kri goats' necks. Unlike the goats, of course, his eyes were pale blue, not amber, and his pupils were round human ones, not vertical slits.

Hippasus shouldn't be alive, not really. Infants with deformities like his were exposed at birth, left to die in the wild. Their mother had defied custom. She knew it was the father's legal right to decide whether or not a child was to live or be exposed, but Adelphos had been away on business the day Hippasus was born. Amethea's mother had held the newborn to her breast and let him suckle, cooed and sang to him. Days later when Adelphos returned, he was livid and ashamed when he saw his son. The divorce came soon after, then the exile to Dia.

Hippasus blinked and seemed startled to see Amethea standing before him.

"Wake up, brother," she said with a burst of impatience. "I've brought you food." She placed a folded leaf that held a serving of chickpeas cooked with wild greens on his rock, along with a heel of barley bread and a handful of plump raisins. He nodded thanks but didn't reach for the food.

Amethea then noticed that Hippasus' right hand was curled into a loose fist as if he were holding something. He slowly opened his fingers and there in the center of his palm sat a small object that looked very much like a large honeybee. It was made from some kind of unusual material she couldn't identify. A special kind of cloth? A thin sheet of hammered gold? No, neither of those.

"What is that, Hippasus?"

"A magic bee," he responded, "from the Bee Maker."

Amethea stared at the origami bee. It wasn't a real, living bee, though it was a good likeness. It even dangled legs that bulged with pollen sacs. She had seen bees embossed on seals and coins as well as bee-shaped beads and earrings before, but this was not the pressed bronze of a coin nor an ornament fashioned from gold leaf. She picked it up and held it carefully between her thumb and forefinger, careful not to crush it. She held it close to her eyes to examine. The material was soft yet firm, light as air. Was it made from a special kind of papyrus? A sudden image of a girl running flashed before her eyes and so startled her, she gave a little cry and dropped the bee back onto her brother's hand. Her grey eyes opened wide. She narrowed her glance as she turned again to her brother.

"Hippasus, where did you find that? Who is the Bee Maker?"

Her brother's face was filled with wonder as if lit from a lamp within. She shivered. Had her brother been visited by a divine being, a nymph or goddess, or Pan himself? Some said the sound of Pan's pipes could plunge a person into madness. Her brother didn't look mad; he looked calm. But her skin erupted in goose bumps. She sensed the strange bee held a rare power and it frightened her.

Hippasus stretched both legs out before him and paused before answering. He seemed to taste and turn his words over before giving them voice, chewing his words the way a goat chews its cud. If Hippasus had turned into a goat on the spot, it wouldn't have surprised her. He was so goat-like! Why couldn't he just answer her the way any other boy might? No wonder he was the brunt of other boys' taunts, "Goat boy! Goat boy!"

Hippasus was silent for so long she feared he had fallen into another spell. She shifted her weight from foot to foot impatiently. If he was like a goat, she was a restless mare.

At last he spoke, "Nymph or goddess, I don't know, Amethea. But she makes bees! I was listening to the shrine bees hum and they allowed me to see Her."

"Who is she?" Amethea asked again, her voice tinged with doubt.

"She was young, Amethea, a maiden like you. She drifted in and out of sight, all wavy as if she was wrapped in sea mist. And she was making bees, folding their bodies from squares of gold and black, placing them in a basket. For an instant, I could see her perfectly clear. Such strange clothes! Then something wriggled in my hand and when I looked down, it was one of her bees and it was moving, alive!"

"But this bee is not alive, Hippasus. It looks like some kind of ornament."

"After it perched on my hand, it fell asleep."

Hippasus gently stroked the origami bee's back. To Amethea's astonishment, the ornament stirred. The wings began to beat and the bee lifted from Hippasus' hand and flew towards the snag that housed the shrine's wild hive. It disappeared into the dark mouth of the hive's entrance. Amethea looked at Hippasus, her eyes a mixture of disbelief and awe.

Solemnly, Hippasus said, "She saw me. Before she disappeared, the Bee Maker looked right at me. I am sure of it." Hippasus closed his eyes. When he opened them again, he whispered, "Do you think it was Artemis?"

Amethea shivered. Was it possible? Bees had welcomed Hippasus at his birth, a sign, their mother always claimed, that he was under the goddess' protection. She waited to see if the ornament bee would return but it did not, and Amethea found herself doubting what she had just seen. She sat down and did what she always did when she needed to collect her thoughts or ease some mounting worry in her breast. She reached into the pouch slung across her back and pulled out her aulos. She lifted the double flute to her lips and began to play while Hippasus ate his barley roll and raisins. What did it mean, her brother's vision of the Bee Maker? Was it an omen? Was the Bee Maker Artemis? Or perhaps Artemis had sent a messenger, a bee nymph, to confirm that Hippasus was her own? Rather than feeling relieved or comforted, Amethea felt uneasy. Doubt gnawed at her. She put down her flutes and watched Hippasus play with his pebbles. Sun glinted on his little horns.

What if Hippasus was not quite human? What if he really was the spawn of a goat-god and able to commune with the hidden gods of the wild fields? That would mean her mother had consorted with or been seduced by Pan or one of his kind, just as Karpos had accused. Was it possible? Perhaps her mother had protected Hippasus out of fear. If Hippasus were the child of Pan, the god would not have taken kindly to the baby being exposed at birth.

Amethea took a deep breath and chided herself. Hippasus was an odd child, physically deformed, at times vexing, but surely he was a human boy, her own brother. They shared the same oval face, high cheekbones, and deep-set eyes of their mother. And only an hour earlier, Karpos had reassured her that he would take Hippasus under his care. The tightness in her chest loosened slightly and she half-laughed at her far-fetched thoughts. All would be well, hadn't Karpos told her that? Amethea placed her aulos back in the pouch and laid her hand gently on her brother's shoulder. He smiled at her, his eyes still lit by the wonder of seeing the Bee Maker, whoever or whatever she was.

All will be well, Amethea repeated softly to herself. Even so, she was unable to entirely suppress a darker, more sinister voice that whispered in her ear. *What good is a Bee Maker to you?* the voice taunted. *You will never race at the Heraea Games. No statue in Hera's Temple will honor you.* She sat down on a low boulder at the edge of the shrine and chewed a few of the raisins Hippasus had left uneaten. She watched him arrange his pebbles into patterns. The raisins tasted bitter to her. High overhead a pair of golden vultures traced wide circles in the cloudless sky. Vultures were death seekers. Perhaps it was the death of her dreams they were after.

Neither sibling was aware of the energetic dance taking place within the hive, how the origami bee excitedly wiggled and waggled, unfolded and refolded itself, as the other bees watched, their bodies vibrating. Nor did Amethea and Hippasus notice when the origami bee emerged from the tree and flew up into the blue sky like a spark of sunshine, then vanished as if pulled through an invisible hole in the firmament. And when they turned to follow the path back home to their cottage, they did not see the origami bee return with a swarm of living honeybees whose faces, if you could read the faces of bees, were filled with the joy of those who have returned after a long, hard absence. The bees disappeared into the snag.

CHAPTER NINE

A HURRICANE
OF HOPE

The last person Melissa expected to see the following morning was Beau, but he appeared with Amaltheia in tow just as Melissa sat down on the cypress bench to fold an origami bee.

"Hola, origamista!"

"What?"

"Hi, Mel."

"I thought you were only suspended for two days." The goat pranced up to her and Melissa placed a hand over her basket to prevent any more bees from becoming a goat snack.

"Uh, it's Saturday."

"Oh, yeah."

Hermes trotted over to Amaltheia and assumed the downward dog do-you-want-to-play stance. The goat bleated, kicked up her dainty hooves, and dog and goat dashed around the yard together.

"Look at that!" Beau crowed.

"I guess they've decided to be friends."

"Think we might do the same?"

"I guess." Melissa tried to focus on her next fold but felt suddenly self-conscious.

Beau sat down beside her. "Still making bees, I see. Is this like folding a thousand peace cranes or something? Because if it is, I'd be glad to help you get there."

Melissa looked at him, half in exasperation and yet half pleased to see him. He wasn't going to quit bugging her; that much was clear. "If you really want to know, I do plan to fold a thousand. It's a surprise for Ba."

Beau looked thoughtful and said, "Like a prayer for his work to bring the bees back."

Beau had surprised her yet again.

"I know it's silly. A bunch of paper bees can't replace the real ones."

"I don't think it's silly. It's beautiful." Beau took out his ball of red clay and divided it into two pieces. In moments he had sculpted a miniature Hermes and Amaltheia that he set on the bench. He wiped his red hands on his cut-offs and took a piece of origami paper.

Just then Melissa's holo-band chirped. She waved a finger over it and received an audio message from Noi. "I'm installing the moth quilts at the Modern Art Museum today so I'll be out of pocket but I keep thinking about your seizures. Call soon, nhé!"

Beau looked at her, a question in his eyes.

"That was my Vietnamese grandmother." Melissa wished Noi hadn't said anything about the seizures. Beau would think she had them all the time.

"She makes quilts?"

"Yeah, she's an artist."

"Cool, what's her name?" Beau stretched out his long legs, then made a crisp fold on his origami square.

"Mechtild Tran."

"Mechtild? That's sounds more German than Vietnamese."

"That's because it is." Melissa placed a completed bee in the basket. She hoped Beau would ignore Noi's comment about seizures.

"Mind explaining?"

"It's a name my Noi—Noi means paternal grandmother — took for herself after seeing a painting of a nun named Mechtild."

"Why would she do that?" Beau flipped his paper over and made another crease.

Melissa explained, "Mechtild was a mystic who lived like a thousand years ago in Germany. When Noi saw the painting, she says she felt so strong a connection, she wept."

"That must be some painting."

"Here, I can bring it up on a holo-vid." Melissa traced a pattern in the air over her holo-band and a copy of the painting rose into the air before them. An abstract figure wearing a nun's dark habit stood with arms flung open as she walked between two trees. The foliage of the trees made her appear surrounded by pale green light as if she had wings.

"She looks like a large, luminous moth," said Beau. "Like a Luna moth."

"She does, doesn't she?"

"So are you a mystic, too?" Beau stopped folding and gave her such a direct look, she blushed.

Fidgeting with her bee's wings, she protested. "Me? No way. I'm the engineering type, a math geek."

"Hey, math like the kind Bella does, can get pretty far out there."

"That's different. Mystics talk about being absorbed into some kind of nameless one-ness. That just sounds scary to me."

"But are your seizures ever like that?"

Melissa shot him an accusing glance. "I don't want to talk about that."

"Why not?"

"Drop it."

How could she explain to him how defective her seizures made her feel? How they stole parcels of her life? How she worried about falling into blankness and never coming out of it, like a honeybee that forgot its way home? Or maybe like a quark blinking out of existence?

"Some famous artists were epileptics," Beau observed.

"You don't know the first thing about it. I hate having seizures so don't make me talk about it."

Hermes trotted up to the bench and she leaned over to bury her face in his black fur. She breathed in his comfortable doggy scent. When she sat back up, Beau was concentrating on a wing fold. She wasn't sure, but he looked like maybe she had hurt his feelings.

"I'm sorry," she said, "it's just that.."

"Don't worry about it," he said. He placed his finished bee in the basket.

"I want to show you something," he said, and pulled a soft tablet shaped like a pencil from his pocket. He unrolled it into a flat screen and tapped it. The screen seemed to come to life as thousands, no millions, of orange and black butterflies swooped gracefully across it

"Are those monarchs?" Melissa asked.

"My Abuelita made this video twenty years ago. When monarchs still migrated. I've been experimenting with my tablet's 3-D and sensory functions to expand the video. Watch."

Melissa sat entranced as monarch butterflies spiraled from the flat screen into the air. An enormous cloud of 3-D monarchs soon surrounded them. They sat in the calm eye of a hurricane made of butterfly wings. Now and then, a butterfly would swoop close in and delicately brush Melissa on the cheek or hand. After several magical moments, the butterflies slowly drifted back down into the screen. Beau rolled the tablet back up into a pencil and tucked it in his pocket.

"The real ones, they're mostly gone now, aren't they?" Melissa said softly.

Beau turned to her. "Do you ever feel really, really angry at how ruined the world is? At how many species humans have killed off?"

"Yeah, I do." Melissa didn't have words for all her feelings.

"But you're folding a thousand origami bees."

"I know. It's stupid. It won't help anything."

"No, I mean, it's beautiful. It's like you have hope."

"Sometimes I'm afraid hoping will only make things worse if nothing works out." She didn't explain to Beau that folding the bees was also about finding a way to connect with her father. And that was pretty hopeless, too.

"But you're still folding the bees."

"Yeah." She was silent for a moment, then added, "I'm glad you're helping."

"Me, too."

CHAPTER TEN

PEBBLES AND POMEGRANATES

Amethea placed her heels on the start line marked with a stone and took a few deep breaths. She was dressed in a plain knee length chiton. Hippasus perched on a large rock to cheer her on. He had devised a way to time her sprints by plucking the strings of his lyre. The fewer the plucks before she crossed the finish line, the faster her pace. Dika had urged her to get out and run again. "It will ease your grief and protect you from fever," she claimed. Dika was a firm believer in fresh air, sun, and exercise to ward off illness. "Your mother would have wanted you to. Your running pleased her."

Amethea ran with abandon, knowing these sprints would likely be her last on Dia. Soon she would join her uncle's household in Larisa and do what was expected of every young woman. Spin and weave long hours each day. But she wasn't in Larisa yet, and though she didn't dare mention anything to Hippasus or Dika, she wanted to believe that Karpos had meant to hint he might take her to the Heraea Games. She must be ready to race! She threw her head back, shook her copper curls loose from her headband, and ran two plunks of the lyre faster than her previous sprint. She collapsed beside Hippasus, her breath coming in rapid bursts, a big grin on her face.

The earth sent coils of energy through Amethea's bare feet that made her feel like a bounding hare. Dika was right, running did lift her spirits. She couldn't help notice, however, that as her own spirits lifted, Hippasus' mood darkened. He spent more and more time alone at the shrine, often refusing to return to the cottage at night to sleep. Finally, she confronted him.

"Hippasus, you spend too much time alone. And anyway, I need you to help me prepare for our move to Larisa. Karpos said you will not need to bring clothes, but we'll pack the inkwell Mother gave you, the one shaped like a beehive. You're fond of it, aren't you?"

"I doubt I will be needing an inkwell, Amethea."

"Of course, you will. Karpos will hire a proper tutor for you."

"Did he say so?"

"I am sure he means to."

"Karpos will take you to live in his fine house, Amethea. Not me."

"Nonsense! He's making arrangements for both of us. It will be a different life than the one we're used to, but we must think of it as an adventure."

Amethea looked at her brother in exasperation. He was a boy; things would go better for him. Couldn't he see that? Hippasus, a male in a family of three daughters, would be favored in her uncle's household. His freedom would expand as hers shrank.

Hippasus picked up his lyre and plucked a string. "Run another length!" he urged.

"I will!"

Amethea was determined to remember every stone and tuft of grass beneath her feet. She wanted to carry Dia in her feet forever, to remember what it felt like to be swift and strong. Soon her daylight hours would be spent indoors and before long, Karpos would choose a husband for her. Her life would be spent spinning and weaving for her family's needs. That was the way of it. But today, today she could run.

As she took her place at the start line, the voice she had tried to suppress hissed in her ear. *If your father had not abandoned you, you could have been a young Atalanta. If Hippasus had been born like other boys.* She bit her lip. Why couldn't she escape these unwanted thoughts? They were like vipers writhing in the pit of her stomach. She tossed her head as if to shake the thoughts away and then ran fast, faster, so fast no thought could follow.

"Another two plucks faster!" crowed Hippasus.

Amethea slowed to a jog to catch her breath. How fast, she wondered, would she need to be to equal Atalanta's pace?

When she sat down beside him, Hippasus surprised her with a question. "Is it true, Amethea, that our father was a great athlete?"

"It's true, Hippasus. But we have no claim on him as father."

"Because of me. Do you blame me for that?"

His question caught her off guard. Had he guessed her darker thoughts? She forced a smile and protested, "Hippasus!

I love you as Mother did. Our father left because he had a restless spirit."

Hippasus straightened out his leg and pointed at his deformed foot. "You don't need to protect my feelings. It's no secret our father divorced Mother after she gave birth to a goat boy."

Amethea detected a tone of bitterness in her brother's voice.

"Who told you that?" she demanded.

"I figured it out for myself. I may have the foot of a beast, but my mind is clear."

"Well, it makes no difference. It changes nothing." Amethea tried putting her arm around his shoulders but he held up a hand to stop her.

"No, Amethea. It makes a very big difference. You will go with Karpos, but he will never accept me." He passed a hand over the bumps on his head, then looked back at Amethea as if daring her to contradict him.

"Karpos gave his word. I've already told you—"

Hippasus lifted his hand again. "I've been thinking, Amethea. Karpos doesn't want me to pollute his household. I can ask Kimon and Dika to let me stay on Dia with them. I can help Kimon with the goats. He can teach me to sculpt."

Amethea stood up, her red curls like flames in the sunlight, and placed her hands on both hips. "Hippasus, do not speak so! I don't think Mother intended you to become the ward of slaves."

"They are freed now, Amethea. Kimon and Dika are like family."

Amethea felt momentarily ashamed for she knew Hippasus was right. Kimon and Dika would never have treated Hippasus the way Karpos had, but Karpos had softened on that last day. He had given his word.

"Karpos will fulfill his obligations as our uncle. I am sure of it." She sat back down and grasped Hippasus' hand to reassure him.

"When he was here, he refused to look at me. He called me a satyr's son. Karpos would be happier if I did not exist."

Amethea frowned. It was true that Karpos had avoided contact with Hippasus, ordered him out of the room. But he would warm up to her brother once he got to know him better.

"I must return home. Will you join me?"

"I want to spend more time in the shrine. I'm working out a new pattern with the pebbles. And I want to be there when the Bee Maker returns."

Hippasus had not spoken of any more visions and Amethea found herself doubting whether the bee had ever come to life in the first place. More likely a breeze had blown it from Hippasus' hand and fooled them both. In fact, she suspected the bee was not a sign from Artemis at all but a clever ornament that Hippasus himself had made, though how or from what material she couldn't guess. It irritated her that he would try to fool her by claiming a vision. Why couldn't he behave like other boys? Karpos would find such strangeness even more galling than his deformed leg and horns.

Impatience rose in her breast. "Play with your pebbles then." She turned and hurried down the path back to the cottage. There she filled a trunk with garments for herself and a few beloved objects including the inkwell her mother had given Hippasus, her dolphin brooches and spindles, a gold and garnet necklace her mother had worn. Most of their household goods—dishes and pots, wine and water jugs—she would leave behind for Dika and Kimon. A sudden rush of tears filled her eyes. Hippasus was right, Kimon and Dika were like family. She would miss them both terribly.

When the sun hung low in the western sky over a lapis lazuli sea, Hippasus slung his lyre over one shoulder, picked up his walking stick, and pushed himself to standing. Dove, as always, walked close beside him in case he needed to lean on her. Hippasus reached into his tunic to make sure the two pomegranates were safely tucked inside. He had plucked them from a small tree that clung to the cliff edge behind the shrine. Pomegranates were Amethea's favorite fruit. Pleased with his gift, he whistled a tune of his own making and did not hear the steps or ragged breathing of the local tanner until the man lunged across the path and blocked his way. Hippasus tried to move aside but the man swayed, lost his balance, and heaved against Hippasus, causing him to stumble. Dove flattened her ears and snarled at the man who staggered back a step.

"Call off your mongrel or I will gut her!" he shouted and reached into his robe to pull out a knife. Hippasus smelled undiluted wine on his breath. The man's hands and arms were stained with oak tannins used to soften animal hides and his body smelled bitter.

"We mean you no harm, Sir. You startled us, that's all."

A line of spittle dribbled down the corner of the tanner's mouth. He jutted his head forward to get a closer look at Hippasus. His beady eyes hardened and he spat.

"Spawn of a goat! You are the demon that killed my son. By the gods, I will take my vengeance!" He lifted his dagger but before he could plunge it into Hippasus, Dove leapt and caught his wrist in her sharp teeth. His knife fell and clattered on stones. Then, to Hippasus' surprise, the man fell over in a heap. Kimon stepped out from behind a bush holding his shepherd's crook. He had given the man a hard knock on the head.

Kimon knelt down and checked the tanner. "Drunkard," he said in disgust. "He will wake with a well-deserved knot on his head."

"You saved my life, Kimon, and you, too, Dove!" The boy's face was drained of color. Dove stood over him protectively.

"I thank Pan for putting my feet on the path at the right moment," Kimon said. Kimon, like his wife, was devoted to Pan, god of shepherds and wild places.

"He said I killed his son, Kimon. Why would he say such a thing?"

Kimon looked at the boy with a mixture of kindness and pity. "The wild rants of a man who has drunk too much, that's all."

"No, it was more than that, Kimon. Why did he think I killed his son?"

Kimon offered his hand to help Hippasus stand up. "Young Master, please, I will accompany you home."

"Not until you tell me what you know."

"Then your sister has not told you of the rumors?"

Hippasus cocked his head. His eyes filled with confusion. "Rumors, Kimon?"

Kimon sighed and laid a hand gently on the boy's shoulder. "The fever has claimed many lives, Hippasus. People look for someone or something to blame."

"They blame me?" Hippasus asked, his young voice trembling in disbelief. "My own mother is dead!"

Kimon lowered his eyes . "Some in the village blame you, not all. Dika has heard the tanner mumble that you are cursed by the gods, that your presence pollutes the island."

"They think my ugliness is the cause of fever?" cried Hippasus. "Do they think I would kill my own mother?" Hippasus struggled to hold back angry tears.

Kimon put his arm around the boy's shoulders and tried to comfort him. "Hippasus, you are different, not ugly. When a nymph gave birth to Pan, she was so shocked by her son's goat feet and horns, she fled. But when his father, the god Hermes, presented him to the gods of Mt. Olympus, they were so delighted, they gave Pan dominion over the most beautiful of wild places."

"But I am not Pan, Kimon. My father is not Hermes."

Kimon looked over the boy's head as if pondering what to say. "No, you are a mortal boy, but perhaps Pan has favored you in some way. Your mother did not recoil from you when you were born and a swarm of honeybees hovered in the doorway to welcome you. Your mother loved you. She believed you were born to a good fate."

Hippasus stroked Dove's back, still fighting back tears. "But what fate is that, Kimon?"

"I don't know. You will have to discover it for yourself, young Master. What I do know is that the fever will not last forever. Time will soften grief and rage. But it would be best if you stayed out of sight as much as possible. This foolish brute of a tanner could have harmed you and there may be others like him."

"Do not tell Amethea about this," Hippasus said. "She has enough to worry about. I will bring her only the good news of pomegranates. He reached into his tunic and showed Kimon the ripe pink globes.

"She will be delighted," Kimon said.

At that moment, a thrush nightingale, hidden in a nearby bush, whistled and rattled as if trying to get their attention.

Hippasus turned and the bird flew from the bush and landed on his shoulder.

"Birds, at least, do not find me monstrous."

To Amethea's surprise, that evening Hippasus refused to touch the fish she had grilled for their dinner, saying, "The honeybees have taught me to forsake eating flesh. The pebbles have shown me a new way of seeing."

"But it's only a fish," Amethea said.

"A fish has a life of its own, as does a bird, or a goat."

"What are you talking about, Hippasus?" she asked. Her heart sank, fearing yet more strangeness from her goat-footed brother.

"The Bee Goddess favors barley cakes and flowers. We must never stain her altar with a sacrificed animal."

"Very well," retorted Amethea, "but I would not turn down my share of the slaughtered ox if I won at the Heraea Games." She slid Hippasus' share of fish onto her own plate and ate it, separating flakes of pale flesh from the delicate bones.

Tension hung in the air between them but vanished the instant Hippasus took out the pomegranates. Amethea clapped her hands and thanked him. She sliced one of the pomegranates open, staining her fingers with the sweet scarlet juice. But as she ate the juicy beads, she couldn't help thinking that even a fruit had blood. Sacrifice came in many forms but the gods always demanded it. She would have to give up running. And Hippasus, what would he have to give?

CHAPTER ELEVEN

QUITTING

The following Saturday Melissa sat alone on the cypress bench in the sticky, late morning heat. She felt like melted sugar on a burnt cinnamon roll. The bee she was folding was too damp to hold a crease. She wiped her hands on her shorts and set the half-completed bee on the bench beside her. Goats on Beau's side of the fence nudged at clumps of dry, brittle plants before slumping beneath the shade of a large oak. A mockingbird, grey and slender, perched on a fencepost close enough for Melissa to see the deep, fierce gold of his eye before he scolded her and flew away.

Beau had left Amaltheia in Melissa's care for the day. The blue-eyed goat and Hermes, now best friends, chased each other, scrambled across the yard and leapt into the air, speaking to each other in barks and bleats. Finally, having tired each other out, they settled down by the cypress bench and curled against each other to nap.

Beau and Rocio had borrowed one of the town's solar vans to attend a food and fiber swap in San Antonio, a two hour drive away, and would be gone all day. Her father, as usual, was on campus even though it was the weekend. Melissa rubbed the slight bump at the bridge of her nose and appraised the growing pile of origami bees in the basket. With Beau's help, she had over four hundred bees, still a long way from a thousand. But while the number of origami bees steadily increased, the Yolo County bees dwindled. Everyday her father returned from work long-faced and discouraged, reporting that more bees had failed to return to the hive. He seemed to grow ever more distant and Melissa felt powerless to reach him.

Melissa let out a long breath. Her hands were tired. The folding seemed pointless. She sifted her hand through the basket and paper rubbing against paper made a soft rustling sound like a breeze through parched leaves. She longed for a real breeze. Then out of the day's stillness and unrelenting heat, a thin breeze caressed her neck like a cool hand and lifted a few strands of her hair. Thankful, she closed her eyes. Without warning, the breeze flared into a brisk wind that overturned the basket and sent several bees skyward. The sound of the flute followed. Melissa stiffened her body in an unsuccessful attempt to ward off the seizure.

"Bee Maker," the boy bowed as he spoke. "I've waited for you!"

She stood before the goat-footed boy at the shrine and without thinking held out her hand. An origami bee flew from her hand to his. He nodded and pointed to a hollow tree and then upwards to the cloudless sky. A long line of bees circled overhead, then swept down and entered the hive one by one.

The boy looked at her and said, "Bees from your realm, Goddess. Come to visit their kin."

What did he mean? Did he think she was a goddess, that she had brought bees with her? She shook her head and opened her mouth to protest, but the boy dipped a wooden spoon into a clay urn and motioned for her to sit beside him on a large flat stone. He spread a spoonful of thick, golden honey on a small cake made of barley flour and poppy seeds and handed it to her. The cake had a wholesome earthy flavor, and the honey a deep, complex sweetness. She felt a quivering sensation as honeybees danced about them in a golden circle. Their oscillating wings made a soft humming. Images passed between her mind and the boy's. She closed her eyes and did not see the young woman that stood several yards away on a path that led to the shrine.

Amethea had lowered her flutes and stared. She did not see Melissa, only her brother offering a honey cake to someone who was not there. A chill ran up and down her limbs. Had Hippasus gone mad or did he see things other mortals could not? Fear seized her and she turned and ran back down the path. What kind of creature was her brother?

Melissa and Hippasus exchanged many layers of thoughts. Then suddenly the boy's eyes lost their sheen and he stared straight ahead as if he could no longer see her. The humming of bees faded and Melissa found herself back on the cypress bench. There were crumbs in her hand and a taste of honey in her mouth. Hermes jumped onto the bench and sniffed her hand. He licked the crumbs and placed a paw in her lap. She still felt a quivering in her body as if she were filled with bees. Amaltheia stood and looked at her, her head tilted.

What is happening to me? Melissa fought a surge of panic. Her seizures were no longer blips of absence but a channel that flung her to an ancient shrine that overlooked a turquoise sea. It was Ancient Greece, she was sure. There a young boy, befriended by bees, arranged pebbles in patterns and his sister played a flute. Images flooded her mind and she was amazed by how much she suddenly knew.

The goat-footed boy was named Hippasus. He had recently lost his mother and for some reason, feared his uncle. He was an epileptic like she was and he seemed to think Melissa was a goddess. His right foot was shaped like a hoof; he had two small knobs on his head, curly brown hair and pale blue eyes. But was he real?

Whatever was going on, Melissa was frightened. She knew that some epileptics suffered hallucinations. Brain signals became so scrambled that a person might experience sights and sounds that did not really exist. She needed to tell her father, get checked by a physician. But what about the crumbs that Hermes had just licked and the taste of honey still in her mouth? She shivered.

The boy can't be real, she reasoned with herself. None of this is real. And if I tell Ba, he'll think I'm losing my mind. Am I? As she debated whether or not to tell her father, it struck her that all her strange seizures had occurred while she was folding origami bees. Was folding bees doing something to her mind? If so, she could stop it, put an end to her hallucinations by not folding any more. She grabbed the basket and hurried up the porch steps. She flung the basket in a corner of her closet and covered it with a quilt, a small one that Noi had sewn. She thought of destroying the bees, building a fire and throwing them into it, but something held her back. The bees had taken hours and hours of effort. She had made them to pray for the bees and to cheer her father. She had folded them because she wanted more than anything to earn her father's affection. And each one, she had to admit, almost felt like a real bee to her, a personality composed of paper.

"But I can't fold any more. I won't," she declared, and brushed her hands in a gesture of finality.

Just then her wristband vibrated and a holographic image of her grandmother appeared. Melissa could see the print of the Mechtild painting on the wall behind Noi, the mystic's arms flung open in a gesture of ecstatic surrender.

"Noi?"

"Melissa, I hope I'm not a bother."

"No, of course not, Noi." Melissa closed the closet door and sat down on her bed.

"But I had a sudden feeling I needed to check in. Have you had any more seizures?"

Melissa stiffened. Her grandmother had an uncanny way of reading her thoughts. "A few, but I'm okay."

"Are you still hearing the flute?"

Melissa didn't want to reveal what had just happened, not even to Noi, but she answered in a small voice, "Sometimes."

Her grandmother peered at her and opened her mouth to speak but hesitated.

"Noi, I'm fine."

Her grandmother turned and pointed to the print of Mechtild. "I often wonder if Mechtild's experiences were related to seizures."

"You mean Mechtild was epileptic, too?" asked Melissa.

"Well, no one knows."

"But you told me that she had experiences of great joy, of feeling one with the universe and all that. That doesn't sound very much like epilepsy."

"A seizure can be a kind of surrender, Melissa, a means to open oneself to greater awareness, and in that awareness, discover joy."

"Noi, I don't want to be a mystic," blurted Melissa. She shifted her body. Epilepsy was a brain disorder, a mix-up of chemical signals. Melissa didn't see how it could possibly be a door to awareness.

Her grandmother picked up a piece of cloth and a threaded needle. "You do not have to be anything, but hating your seizures doesn't help, does it?"

Melissa didn't answer. She half longed to tell Noi about Hippasus, but fear held her back.

"Noi, I've always wondered about something."

"Yes?"

"Mechtild was a Christian mystic. She believed in God."

Noi nodded. "And you're surprised that a Buddhist like me who does not, would feel deep kinship with one who does?"

"Sort of."

"It's true I'm not attracted to the idea of an all powerful deity but I do feel wonder and gratitude for the vast web of being and for every unique creature on that web. Mechtild's God and my web may well be the same thing."

"That makes sense, I guess." Melissa silently debated with herself. Should she tell Noi about the visions? Was the goat boy a creature on Noi's web or a figment of Melissa's epileptic brain?

Her grandmother gave her another probing look. "Little bee, you'll contact me if your seizures increase or change?"

"Really, Noi, I'm fine."

"Well, I've got to harvest a bitter melon to make soup tonight. I hand pollinate my melon vines now. It's quite a nuisance and often not successful. Keep folding those origami bees and help your Ba bring our honeybees back, nhé!"

Melissa thought of the trellis on Noi's narrow apartment balcony and the slender vines with pale green melons. Each melon was covered with little bumps that reminded Melissa of iridescent opals. Noi had once told her that bitter tastes nourished the heart. That was odd, Melissa thought, because she was pretty sure bitter feelings had the opposite effect. But maybe with the right attention, a bitter feeling could be transformed and somehow make the heart more open, more accepting than it had been before.

Her grandmother's image faded and Melissa went out to sit on the porch swing. She swung back and forth, agitated and torn. She had always shared her troubles freely with Noi but something held her back this time, as if sharing what was happening to her would give the seizures more power. She feared becoming trapped in that other world where the goat boy dwelled. She was afraid of losing herself.

The next day, Sunday, Beau's mother invited Melissa over to show her how to use a spinning wheel. Melissa was grateful to have something to help take her mind off the seizures and when she sat down at the spinning wheel she noticed a new clay figure on an adjacent shelf. It was a girl sitting on a bench folding an origami bee. Melissa smiled and touched it lightly with her finger. Another surprise from Beau.

After the spinning lesson, Rocio served bowls of vegetarian tortilla soup flavored with tiny chile pequin peppers and freshly chopped cilantro. Rocio topped each bowl of steaming broth with crisp tortilla strips and melted goat cheese.

"This is delicious!" Melissa exclaimed.

"Abuelita's recipe," said Beau.

After dinner, Melissa helped Beau wash the dishes. He pretended to fold the dishcloth in his hand and asked, "Bring any origami paper? We could fold some bees."

"No, I forgot," she lied. She hadn't folded any bees since banning the basket to her closet.

On Monday, Beau stopped by after school. He leaned his bike against the fence while Hermes leapt about him, clutching a knotted rope in his teeth. Beau tossed it high in the air several times for Hermes to catch then joined Melissa on the porch.

"Want some iced tea?" she asked.

"Sure, and then I can help you fold some bees."

Melissa poured Beau a tumbler of tea. "Let's do something else for a change. It's too hot and sweaty for origami."

"Okay, but we're still a long way from a thousand."

"Yeah," countered Melissa, "actually, I think we've folded enough. I'm kind of tired of it."

Beau's eyebrows arched in surprise. "I thought you made a vow to fold a thousand."

"Sheesh, Beau, it's not like I swore on a Bible," Melissa snapped.

Beau looked at her quizzically. "Sorry, just wanted to help. If you don't want to fold any more bees, that's your business."

As they rocked on the porch swing, Melissa watched Beau model a miniature Hermes, roll the clay back into a ball, then begin to model a goat.

"I will be so glad when school is over," he said. "I can't believe the homework my math teacher came up with."

"What do you mean?" Melissa took a sip of her own tea.

"She's always trying to give us 'fun' things to stretch our brains." Beau curled the first two fingers of both hands into quotations marks for the word 'fun.' Some stuff has been sort of interesting, like Fibonacci numbers—you'd have liked that. Did you know that the family tree of a honeybee follows a Fibonacci sequence?"

"Yeah, I did."

"Oh right, I was forgetting you're the math geek daughter of a honeybee scientist."

Melissa gently punched Beau's shoulder. "So what home-work did she give you that was so sadistic?"

"We're supposed to figure out why the numbers 6, 28, and 496 are called perfect numbers without looking it up on our holo-vids."

"I can help. Ba told me about perfect numbers just a few weeks ago. Think about factors. What are the factors of six?"

"Uh, one times six, two times three."

"Throw away the six and add the others."

"Okay. They add to six."

"There you have it."

"Wait, you mean a number is perfect if its factors add up to the number itself?"

"That's it."

"You're a life saver, Mel."

"Since you're such a Greek geek, did you know Pythagoras knew about the first three perfect numbers?"

"I'm more into Phidias than Pythagoras."

Melissa took another sip of iced tea and leaned back and looked up at the porch eaves where a pair of paper wasps was busy building a nest. The paper cells of their silvery-grey nest were hexagons. Another insect engineer.

"So what did Pythagoras do with perfect numbers, anyway?" asked Beau.

"I don't know, but Ba said that Pythagoras practically worshipped numbers." It occurred to Melissa that maybe Numbers were Pythagoras' version of Noi's web or Mechtild's God.

"Well, if I had lived in Ancient Greece, I would have been a sculptor like Phidias, not a mathematician."

Melissa shoved Beau's arm again. "Math is cool, Mr. Valenzuela."

"And so is origami, Ms. Bùi."

Melissa frowned.

"So, what's up?" Beau asked.

"What do you mean?" Melissa turned away from Beau's gaze.

"Why don't you want to fold any more bees?"

Melissa shrugged. "I'm just tired of folding the same thing over and over."

"But I thought you wanted to surprise your father. I thought it was about hope. You don't strike me as a quitter."

"Folding a bunch of bees isn't going to bring any of them back. Ba wouldn't care, anyway. It was all a stupid idea."

"I'd be pretty impressed if someone folded me a thousand bees."

"He cares about real bees, Beau. Paper ones are useless."

"I'd almost say you were scared of something."

"Don't be ridiculous." Melissa jumped up from the porch swing.

"I'm pretty good at reading people, Mel." He placed a hand on her arm but she shook it off and walked to the other end of the porch.

She turned and looked at him. "Drop it, okay?"

Just then they heard the sound of bicycle wheels over gravel and looked up to see Melissa's father coast into the backyard. He stepped off his bike and turned towards the teens, his expression grave.

"Bad news. The only bees left in the Yolo hive are the queen and maybe a hundred worker bees. They won't live much longer without the rest of the colony."

"Where'd all the other bees go?" asked Beau.

"That's just it," he responded. "Our team and a host of student volunteers have scoured nearby fields, woods, even the riverbank, and we haven't found one Yolo bee. It's as if they dissolved in thin air." He ran his fingers through his black hair and adjusted his glasses.

Beau squashed the ball of clay in his hands. "That's bad."

Melissa sat stunned. An image of the bees she had seen during her last seizure flashed across her mind. Hippasus' words came back to her. *Bees from your realm, Goddess. Come to visit their kin.* Was that where the Yolo bees had gone? Was that even possible?

CHAPTER TWELVE
QUANTUM ORIGAMI

She was flying over a turquoise sea tracing wide, graceful circles like a golden brown vulture. Below, dolphins leapt in arcs over white-tipped waves. She was not alone. The goat boy, arms spread and legs stretched behind him, was flying beside her. His stunted horns gleamed in the sunshine. The air was speckled with gold flecks that made a whirring sound. Melissa scooped a handful and blew on them. The flecks became bees, each with a unique face that she recognized. They flew together, Melissa, the goat boy, and the bees, and then dove back down to earth towards the little shrine.

The bees perched on the cube of rose-colored marble and she and the boy began to count them. But as they counted, the bees began to cry. Some fell onto their sides, curled up, and died. Alarmed, Melissa reached into her pocket and pulled out a pack of origami paper. Her fingers moved with impossible speed as she folded bee after bee. She had to replace the ones dying. She was running out of time. She couldn't fold them fast enough.

With a start, Melissa woke. Her room was dark; the sun had not yet risen. She crept from her bed to the closet and pulled aside the quilt that covered the basket of bees. For a long time she sat on the floor cradling it. The Yolo bees needed her, but what must she do?

She felt an urge to run as if she could outrun her sadness and confusion. In the velvet darkness a mockingbird sang as she hurriedly pulled on a sports bra and a pair of shorts. She slipped on a pair of running shoes and whispered, "Come on, boy," to Hermes. He jumped up and wagged his short, blunt tail and gave a quick, excited bark.

"Shh, Hermes, you'll wake Ba." Melissa slipped quietly out of the house, unlatched the gate, and started to jog alongside the road with Hermes beside her. The half moon was a soft milky white and a few white-tailed deer were beginning to stir. Running in Texas humidity, heavy as a wool blanket, had taken some getting used to on her morning runs.

Her street, Horsemint Lane, led past Beau's place and continued on to the college campus, a mile away. She followed that route now. Girl and dog slipped into an effortless rhythm. Melissa's strides were long and even and Hermes kept pace with her, though he stopped every so often to sniff a clump of weeds or a stone, his way of gathering the neighborhood news. The air held the mossy smell of the nearby river as well as a lingering fragrance of skunk, bitter and sharp. A few bats, wrapping up a night of insect gorging, darted overhead.

When she reached campus, Melissa turned around and ran back past her own house as light slowly seeped into the sky. Horsemint Lane in this direction led to the town's public library, a solid two-story building built of Hill Country granite. A few of the original hand-blown glass windows were still intact. Solar panels lined the roof.

At the library, Melissa paused to let Hermes sniff the bike rack and uttered a quick scold when he lifted a leg to leave his scent. One of the library's original panes framed a blurry reflection of the setting moon. To the east, the sky turned silver and pink at its edges. Bats swooped overhead, returning to bat houses beneath the library's eaves.

As Melissa jogged back home, she was filled with a sense of warm kinship. Kinship with moon and deer. With bats and even acrid smelling skunk. It was like Noi's web. Then as she reached her own house, she noticed a light briefly flicker from a window over at Beau's. Beau. He had sensed she was scared about something. She felt a sudden urge to tell him everything, but he would think she was crazy. He'd never understand.

Her father was still asleep when Melissa and Hermes slipped back into the house. Clutching a pack of origami paper, Melissa lifted Hermes into her bike basket and hopped on. The lavender field was pulling her like a magnet. The rising sun spread pink fingers across the sky as she pedaled past Beau's house. He startled her by pulling up beside her on his own bike as if he'd been waiting for her.

In answer to her surprised look, he said, "I was up early to milk the goats and saw you and—"

"Don't you have to get ready for school?" she said.

"Not this early. Don't you want me to come with you?"

"You don't even know where I'm going."

"I don't care."

"I have to do this by myself."

"Are we friends or not?"

"Yes, but—"

"If we're friends, you should tell me what's going on."

"If you really want to know, Beau, I'm losing my mind."

"What?!" Beau pointed at the packet of origami paper in Melissa's bike basket and said, "I thought you didn't want to fold any more."

Melissa groaned. "Geez, Beau, are you some kind of detective?"

"Mel, I just want to help."

Melissa gave an exasperated sigh. "Alright, come along if you want. Just don't ask even one question."

They pedaled silently side by side and quickly reached the college campus. They parked their bikes at a rack and Beau followed as Melissa walked past a stone clock tower and sleepy residence halls to the west side of campus. There she led him on a rocky, root-studded path through a tangle of small trees. Wild grapevines and ball moss clung to branches; lichens formed lacy crusts on others. The path led to the lavender field where their eyes met a sea of purple in the early morning light. Native wildflowers grew alongside the lavender bushes. Horsemint, verbena, and basket flower were in bloom, though many appeared thirsty. Here and there, flower heads drooped; leaf tips looked as if they'd been singed. Nonetheless, it was easy to see that the field was a honeybee paradise. Already awake, industrious bees zigzagged the field and nuzzled flowers for nectar. The air pulsed with their buzzing.

Melissa knew exactly where to find the Yolo County hive at one end of the field, for she had been with her father when he placed it there. She led Beau to it now. No bees were flying in and out of the Yolo hive. Melissa thought of the lonely queen within and felt a sudden stab of sorrow.

She and Beau sat down on a large flat rock located a few yards from the hive. It was sprinkled with black lichen as if someone had stood over it with a pepper grinder. Hermes lay down between them, his ears pricked and nose wriggling.

"Beau," Melissa said, "I'm going to fold origami bees. I might have a seizure."

Beau's eyes questioned hers but he nodded. "I'll be right here, Mel."

She took a deep breath and began to fold, doing her best to tamp down the fear that rose in her chest. After several minutes, a completed bee sat on her palm. Nothing happened. She picked up another square of paper. Beau worked a ball of clay, glancing up now and again. Melissa shifted her awareness to the bees in the field and let her fingers fold on their own. She knew these folds by heart, knew them as well as she knew the eight whorls on her own fingertips. She watched a bee's black and amber striped body wiggle in and out of a blossom. Early sunlight flashed on its narrow, quivering wings. She folded a third bee, then a fourth and a fifth. Her hearing sharpened and she felt her own pulse match the throbbing rhythm of nearby bees. A deep, swaying calm enfolded her as she started to fold a sixth bee. To her half-closed eyes, the field became a pattern of vivid colors that looked like broken glass in a kaleidoscope. Was that how bees saw the world?

Then, as if from a great distance, the sad strains of Amethea's aulos called to her. Her muscles tensed, but she willed her body to give in. Beau looked up to see Melissa staring blankly ahead.

"Mel?"

She didn't respond. Beau looked at her for a long moment and then began to mold her features in his ball of clay.

Melissa felt a floating, unsettling sensation that sent tingles down her arms followed by a tightening in her chest and a quickening of her pulse. Panic engulfed her and she felt on the verge of fainting. But then she saw, emerging from a veil of mists, the boy approaching from the other end of the field. He used a walking stick and was accompanied by a slender, blond hound. Rings of honeybees flew about him making him look like a small Saturn. As if from a great distance, Melissa heard Hermes bark, but she could no longer see him or Beau.

When the boy stood only a few feet away, she saw that his free hand was cupped around something as if to protect it. When he was close enough for her to see what he held, he opened his hand to reveal an origami bee. He looked up at her, his pale eyes holding admiration and awe. She stretched out her hand to touch the bee and the bee began to quiver. It flew up and hovered in the air between them. The honeybees that orbited the goat-footed boy stretched into a long, undulating line and followed the origami bee as it circled the Yolo hive. Then, a few dozen at a time, bees broke away from the circle and flew into the hive. The boy emptied a pouch of pebbles on the ground and began to arrange them in patterns. The blond hound lay down next to the rock and for an instant, Melissa thought she could see a quivering image of Hermes. Were the dogs exchanging a greeting?

Hippasus sat down beside her on the rock and, like before, a channel opened between them. He mentioned his sister again, telling Melissa how she loved to run.

"Mel, look! Can you hear me? Do you see what I'm seeing?!" An excited Beau leapt to his feet and watched in amazement as a long line of honeybees emerged from thin air and entered the Yolo hive.

Melissa did not respond. Beau sat back down and tried to model Melissa in his ball of clay but put it aside as more and more lines of bees materialized. Hermes laid his head in Melissa's lap and whined softly.

"You see the bees, too, don't you, Hermes?" Beau said, then added, "Don't worry, boy, she'll be back."

An hour passed before the long lines of Yolo bees flew back out of the Yolo hive. To Beau they seemed to disappear in mid-air as they flew up, popping out of sight the same way they had popped into it. Like quarks, popping in and out of existence.

But Melissa saw them gather again in circles around Hippasus as she listened to the boy's thoughts. *I do not know what place this is, Bee Maker, but the bees tell me they are sick and afraid here. I will take them back to your shrine on the cliff. There they will find healing in your sacred place.* He stood up and turned to leave.

Wait! Melissa directed her thoughts to the boy. *I am not a goddess. We need our honeybees here.* But the line of communication between her and the boy snapped. *Please don't take them* her thoughts begged as the limping boy, his slender hound, and the bees were sucked back into the void from which they had emerged. Melissa sat staring at the air where the boy had stood. Gradually she grew aware of a gentle pressure on her shoulder and looked up to see Beau.

"Mel, you're back! You won't believe this, but while you were out, a whole flock of bees materialized out of thin air. They flew into the Yolo hive and were dancing up a storm in there. Then they flew out and pfft! they vanished."

Melissa placed a fingertip on the bridge of her nose and took a deep breath to dispel the wooziness she felt. "I don't think a swarm of bees is referred to as a flock."

"That's the goat farmer in me talking. Mel, are you okay? You were out a really long time."

Melissa took another deep breath. She couldn't keep these experiences to herself anymore. She needed to tell someone, someone she trusted. In a hesitant voice, she said, "The boy, he came to me this time. The Yolo bees are with him."

"What boy, Mel?" Beau looked confused.

"I see things, Beau. A different world."

"Maybe you should start from the beginning."

By the time Melissa had finished describing the first time she heard the flute in the almond orchard to the arrival of Hippasus and the Yolo bees, the sun was high in the sky.

Beau whistled. "And you said you weren't a mystic."

"I'm not, Beau. I'm scared. In fact, I hate this! I didn't ask for any of this."

"But can you help get the Yolo bees back?"

"I don't know! I don't know what I'm supposed to do. I was folding bees to save them, not send them away!"

"But they came back just now."

"And left again. They must hate our world, Beau. It's poison for them."

They walked silently back through the thicket, across campus, and to their bikes. Melissa lifted Hermes into his basket and turned to Beau.

"Will you get in trouble for skipping school today?"

"Nah, today was Field Day followed by an ice cream making party. I delivered the goat milk for it yesterday."

"Oh, Beau, I'm sorry."

"Don't be. Being with you today is way more exciting. But what about you? Won't your father wonder where you've been?"

"Are you kidding? He won't even notice I was gone. He leaves for work super early. We're lucky he didn't come out to the meadow while we were there."

"But, Mel, you have to tell him about all this."

Melissa straddled her bike. "No way! He'll think I'm nuts."

Beau shook his head. "I stand as witness if you want to tell him and Bella. I saw the bees, Melissa, I saw them."

Melissa shook her head. "Nobody will believe us."

Beau hopped on his bike. "With his hoof and knobs on his head, your boy sounds a bit like Pan. And the way you describe the flutes and their garments, it definitely sounds like Ancient Greece."

"I know. Wait! " Melissa leaned over and grabbed Beau by the shoulders, nearly falling off her bike. He steadied her as she blurted, "The boy's sister must be Amethea! He said his sister liked to run. He's Amethea's brother, Beau!"

"Ame who?"

"The girl who plays the flute is the girl my mother found!" Melissa hurriedly tapped her holo-band and showed Beau the bronze figurine.

"Holy Zeus, Mel. You're travelling back in time to where your Mom's dig is at?"

"This is too crazy. I'm scared, Beau."

Beau was silent for a moment, then quietly said, "Maybe an epileptic brain is more sensitive, more open to seeing other dimensions. Maybe you're like a honeybee, Mel."

"What, you think honeybees are epileptics? I hate being epileptic, Beau."

"So what makes you think the boy's sister is Amethea?"

"Hippasus told me that she loves to run. The night I first heard the flute was the same night my Mom sent me her image. It feels like there must be some kind of connection."

"Could your Mom help with all this? Sounds like she's somehow part of it."

Melissa shook her head. "I can't tell her, Beau, she'll just think I'm making things up to get her to come home. Or that I've flipped out completely."

Beau reached over and gently squeezed her shoulder. "I don't think you're crazy."

Melissa blinked back tears. "Let's just go home," she said.

They hadn't pedaled far when they saw Amaltheia trotting towards them, looking supremely pleased . "Great, she's broken through another lock," said Beau.

Before Melissa could stop him, Hermes leapt from his basket and ran to cover the goat's face with kisses. He refused to be put back in his basket and so Amaltheia and Hermes trotted alongside the bikes. Back on Melissa's porch, Beau pressed her again. "You're sure you don't want to talk to your Dad or Bella?"

"They won't believe me, Beau. Honeybees and quarks are one thing, but me travelling to Ancient Crete?"

"But you're definitely making something happen when you fold your bees. It's like you're able to fold other dimensions into your origami. This is more than regular seizures, don't you think? Maybe you're rearranging quarks like Bella says the bees do and it's creating some kind of time travel map."

"That's crazy, Beau." Melissa entered the kitchen and poured two glasses of water. She handed one to Beau.

"Yeah, but what if? Isn't origami already kind of magic, the way a flat piece of paper gets transformed into a three-dimensional object? Why not an origami that folds other dimensions into itself?"

Melissa considered Beau's words. As improbable as it all seemed, it did make a bizarre kind of sense. "Well, whatever is happening, the Yolo bees are still missing and I don't know what to do."

"They'll come back, Mel. You'll find a way. Listen, Bella says a bowl of goat milk ice cream helps her think."

"I'm sorry, Beau. You could be eating ice cream. Instead you're wasting your day with me, a raving lunatic."

"You know what? We can make our own. I'll run back home for an ice cream maker and a gallon of goat milk."

"You just don't get it, do you, Beau?"

"Get what?"

But Beau didn't think she was crazy. He said he'd seen the bees himself.

Melissa made an effort to smile. "We could flavor the ice cream with honey," she offered. "Ba brought home a small jar the other day."

"That's one thing they didn't have in Ancient Greece," said Beau as he hopped off the porch and leapt over the fence.

"Honey? They had plenty of honey."

"No, ice cream!" he shouted over his shoulder. The goats scattered as he dashed across the meadow. Melissa watched him, shaking her head.

CHAPTER THIRTEEN

BETRAYAL

Melissa gave Hermes a quick bath, watered the pots of wilting herbs, and turned the hose on herself for a few seconds. She sat on the cypress bench to dry off then picked up a square of origami paper. Her plan wasn't working. She hadn't had another seizure in days although she'd been folding nearly nonstop. Her whole life she'd hated her seizures. Now when she needed one, wanted one—nothing.

Beau stopped by after school. "Any luck?" he asked, then added, "Stupid question. From the look on your face, the answer is a big nada."

Melissa threw her hands into the air. "I used to dread seizures and now when I need one, nothing happens. Beau, I've got to get the Yolo bees back."

Beau sat down beside her and picked up a bee. "Maybe you're trying too hard. I'm on my way to deliver feta cheese to the librarian. Want to come? Might be good to take a break."

Melissa hesitated, then put down the bee she was folding. "Okay. Nothing else is working."

They rode their bikes to the library. When they entered its wide oak doors, it was cool and dark inside as if they'd entered a cave. Beau handed some jars to the librarian sitting at her desk. She was middle-aged and had a long silver braid. She wore a white tank top with an image of a rattlesnake on it. She thanked Beau and turned her gaze back to a holo-screen. The front room was filled with holo-vid screens, but the adjoining room housed old-fashioned paper books and that's where Beau led Melissa. She liked the musty, antique smell of the books. Beau pulled a book from a shelf, a volume on Greek myths.

"Wonder how I missed this. I've been here a thousand times."

The librarian looked up. "That one?" She spoke with a slight twang. "Came in last week, donation from an estate sale over in Vanderpool."

Beau flipped through the pages until he came to a passage that caught his attention. "Check this out, Mel. Ever hear about the Thriai?"

"I don't think so."

"It says here that they were bee nymphs, companions to the god Hermes. They divined the future by casting pebbles on the ground."

Melissa stared at Beau. "Hippasus," she whispered, "makes patterns with pebbles."

Beau whistled. "Are you thinking what I am?"

"Well, according to your theory, which is pretty darn crazy, my origami opens some kind of time travel path. So,"

"maybe pebbles do the same for Hippasus."

"And that somehow links him to me."

Beau's green eyes sparkled. He reached out and gave her hand a quick squeeze. Melissa lifted a finger and lightly touched the bump at the bridge of her nose and considered what Beau was suggesting.

"I don't know, Beau. What if it's not time travel at all and I'm just hallucinating?"

"But what if it is time travel?"

Just then, they heard the voices of other kids coming downstairs from the library's second floor. Melissa slipped behind the stacks.

"Hi, Beau." That was a girl's voice.

"Hey, man." A boy's.

"How come you weren't at field day?" a different girl asked.

"You missed the best part, Beau. That cold delicious ice cream." The first girl again.

Melissa peeked around the stack and saw three teens standing with Beau. The first voice belonged to a girl with wiry pink hair pulled back in a ponytail. She was wearing a striped tank top over short shorts. She had long, well-toned legs. Maybe she was a runner. Melissa felt a little snake of jealousy uncoil, and then fear. What would Beau tell them?

"Yeah, I wasn't feeling well. Bad luck, huh?"

"Or were you making your own luck again?" the other boy teased. "You weren't suspended again, were you?"

"No way."

"Hey," the second girl said, "the movie starts in five minutes. Want to join us, Beau? We're headed to the holo-theater over on campus."

"No thanks."

"It's sci-fi."

"I've got enough sci-fi going on in my own life right now."

Melissa stiffened. Was Beau going to tell them about her secret?

"What do you mean?"

"Chupacabra sightings!"

"No way!"

Beau laughed. "Just kidding. Actually, I've got goat chores."

"Too bad," the first girl said.

"Okay, see you around." The boy.

"See ya."

Melissa waited until she heard the library door open and close before joining Beau by the bulletin board.

"Friends of yours?"

"Just kids I know. I would have introduced you, but—"

"Actually I'm glad you didn't."

"Not ready to make your grand entry into Benefit society?" he teased.

She punched him lightly on the arm. "There's too much going on right now. You know."

"Yeah, I do." He pointed at a bulletin board and said, "Hey look, the college is sponsoring a 5K race along the river trail on Sunday. Three days from now. You should enter."

Melissa barely glanced at the flyer. "This is hardly the time for a race," she protested. "And anyway, I'm out of racing shape."

"Are you kidding? I've seen you sprint by my place in the mornings with Hermes. And I think it's the perfect time for a race. It'll help take your mind off things."

Melissa hesitated. It did sound like fun. Folding origami bees wasn't helping her reach Hippasus or retrieve the Yolo bees. Maybe a race would help shake things up.

The librarian looked up from her desk and said, "I can sign you up right now, if you like. The library is co-sponsor. It's a benefit for the bee sanctuary."

Beau and Melissa stared at each other and Beau raised an eyebrow. "Bella gets so wrapped up in her work she forgets to mention basic things. Your Dad, too, I think."

Unable to convince Beau to sign up with her, Melissa said, "Okay, but I expect you to cheer me on. Ba never goes to my races."

"You're kidding. Why not?"

"Too busy. Not interested."

Beau gave her a concerned look and then gave her shoulder a quick squeeze.

"Well, I'll bring Amaltheia and Hermes and the three of us will whoop it up when you cross the finish line."

"I just hope it's less than 110 degrees on Sunday morning."

"Actually, they're predicting rain," added the librarian. "Hopefully no more than a light shower at race time, though Lord knows we could use a good drenching. The river's awfully low."

The sea was a pale blue stippled with white flakes of sunlight the morning Karpos returned to Dia. Unknown to Amethea, he visited with members of the Dia Council before climbing the path to her cottage. She recognized the heavy, impatient sound of his footsteps and came out to greet him in the courtyard. She set out a cup of diluted wine and a dish of sesame seed honey balls. Karpos plucked a rose from the trellis. He crushed the white petals in his hand, inhaled their perfume, and then tossed the bruised petals on the ground.

"It is a good day," he announced.

Amethea invited him to sit at the small table and then stood across from him. She smiled nervously. Would he mention anything about the Heraea Games? She dropped the spindle in her hand and began twisting strands of wool into thread while Karpos drank his wine.

"Your thread is fine and even," he said. "My wife will be pleased."

"When do we leave for Larisa, Uncle?"

"If all goes well, we will depart in five days time. I have found a buyer for the cottage and need some days to tie up business. You are not impatient, niece?"

"No, Uncle." Secretly, she was glad. A few more days meant she could fit in more runs on her beloved Dia.

"Where is Hippasus?" Karpos asked, looking around.

Amethea's heart lifted. It was good to hear Karpos call her brother by his proper name. Encouraged, she said, "I apologize he's not here to greet you. He's out tending the goats with Kimon."

"A pity. I would have liked to see him. I have news for him, as well."

Encouraged even more, Amethea said, "Uncle, Hippasus and I are excited he will have a chance for proper studies. Mother gave him an inkwell in the shape of a beehive and was teaching him his alphabet."

"Studies?" Karpos wrinkled his face as if he'd tasted something foul.

"You will find him a tutor, won't you, Uncle?"

"Tutor for a goat-boy?!" Karpos burst out laughing, then eyed Amethea shrewdly. "Amethea, I'm afraid you have misunderstood me. Hippasus will not be coming to Larisa with us."

His words hit Amethea like a stone. "Not coming with us, Uncle? But I thought—"

"Niece, I assured you that he would be taken care of."

The words 'taken care of' suddenly held an ominous ring.

"You intend him to stay on Dia with Kimon and Dika?"

"Fostered by freed slaves? Nonsense. No, Hippasus has an overdue debt to pay."

A passing cloud shadowed Karpos' face. Amethea felt a sudden chill.

"Debt, Uncle? He is a child. What debt can he owe?"

"Amethea, you must have known this was coming."

Amethea turned from her Uncle's cold gaze. She wanted to flee. She did not want to hear what he was about to say.

"In any case," Karpos said between mouthfuls of wine and sesame seeds, "it is out of my hands. The Council reached their decision this morning and I gave my full consent. It was the righteous thing to do."

"What are you saying, Uncle? Consent to what?" Amethea felt a rising panic.

"Hippasus will be offered as a sacrifice."

Amethea's eyes widened like those of a frightened mare. She looked at Karpos in horror and disbelief. "What do you mean 'sacrificed?" She threw her spindle on the table.

Karpos rose from the table, slapped her, and pressed the spindle back into her hand. "Comport yourself, niece," he growled. "He is not to be put to death like some common criminal. His death will be noble. He will die to end the fever."

Amethea lifted a hand to her stinging cheek, hot tears welling in her eyes. She could barely follow Karpos' next words.

"Two elders will come for Hippasus tomorrow morning. You must not tell him why. It would be unwise to frighten the boy. No, let him think they have invited him to a banquet. I had hoped to tell him about the invitation myself."

"Invite the goat boy to a banquet? You expect him to believe that?"

Karpos cleared his throat and stroked his beard. "The gods must be placated. It would have been kinder for your mother to expose Hippasus at birth. Had she obeyed your father, obeyed me, there would be no fever now. Your brother is a pollution. Let him accept his fate."

"But he is no more than a boy!" Amethea protested. "Cretans are a civilized people. We do not sacrifice human beings!"

"He is not human. He is half-goat," Karpos retorted, "a satyr's bastard."

"You can't believe that!" Amethea cried. "Hippasus has a misshaped foot, that's all. He's not the first person born a cripple."

"And how do you explain the horns on his head?" Karpos stood up and loomed over her. "Can we be sure you yourself do not bear a satyr's marks? You picked up the flute before you could even walk. Was that at Pan's bidding?"

Her uncle's tone was menacing and a cold fear washed over Amethea. Would he bring a case against her, too? "Uncle," she stammered, then dropped to her knees and flung her arms around his legs. He shoved her away and commanded, "Get up, niece. I do not accuse you, but you place yourself in danger if you oppose your brother's sacrifice."

Amethea bent her head as bitter tears fell.

"Do not warn Hippasus." Karpos yanked her up and forced her to sit down. "Do not weep. Yield to the will of the gods." Karpos leaned over and placed his bearded cheek close to her own. "Obey me, Amethea," he said in a hoarse whisper.

Amethea's mind went numb. Neither spoke for several moments. At last she picked up her spindle and began to drop it again. Drop and twist, wind the thread. Her hands shook. How would they kill Hippasus? Slit his throat the way they would a goat's? For an instant she imagined plunging her spindle like a knife into Karpos' chest, but then felt the fight drain from her limbs like blood from a butchered animal. Her spindle dropped to the ground with a dull thud.

"You have today," said Karpos. "Call Hippasus home. Roast a lamb. Play his favorite tunes on your aulos. Make his last hours pleasant ones."

"He will refuse meat," was all she said.

Karpos placed a hand on her shoulder. "Accept the Council's decision, Amethea. Accept the will of the gods, and I promise I will take you to the Heraea Games this summer. You will place your victory statue next to your mother's in the temple of Hera."

His words were like a splash of cold water. She stared at him, confused.

"You are young, inexperienced," he continued in a voice that was almost tender. He stroked her cheek. "But the Games will make you strong, young Atalanta."

"You mean to take me to the Games, Uncle?"

"But the sacrifice of Hippasus must come first."

The hissing voice that she had tried so hard to silence in recent days now took command. *Victory! You were meant for this, Amethea. You were meant for this, young Atalanta.*

An image of herself dashing to a win at the Heraea Games flashed in her mind. To earn victory at the Games! This was an anchor to hold on to, wings to fly by, a way to ease the horror of Hippasus' death. The roar of the stadium crowds filled her ears. Like the drumming of a million cicadas flying on wings of woven light. Who was she to question the way of the gods? Hippasus must die. She must race.

Amethea lifted her head to look at Karpos and then bowed it again. "I accept this, Uncle."

"You are wise." Karpos joined his palms together. "You have a true athlete's heart, Amethea. Didn't Atalanta harden her heart as suitor after suitor met his doom? You must harden yours for one death only. And then victory shall be yours."

"And the fever will end?" she asked, her voice trembling.

"The fever will end."

CHAPTER FOURTEEN

SACRIFICE

The seizure finally came. Melissa slipped into it the next afternoon as she and Beau were folding origami bees. Beau waited anxiously. When Melissa emerged from the seizure, her face twisted in horror.

"What's wrong?" Beau asked. "Did you find the Yolo bees?"

"They're going to kill him," she said.

"Kill the bees?"

"Hippasus. They're going to sacrifice him. He's just a little boy, but they're going to drown him." Melissa felt sick to her stomach.

"What do you mean? Why would anyone want to drown him?"

Melissa looked down at her hands and saw an origami bee there, perfect and whole. In sudden exasperation, she crumpled the paper insect and threw it on the ground.

Beau bent down to pick it up and started to smooth out the paper, but Melissa grabbed his arm and shook her head. "What's the point, Beau? Hippasus is going to die. The Yolo bees will never return. My origami can't help a thing."

Beau put a hand on her arm. "Maybe you have these visions because there's something you can do."

"What? What can I do?" Melissa shook his hand off then grabbed a handful of bees from the basket and threw them into the yard. "I can't fold any more. I just can't."

"At least tell me what you saw." Beau said.

"I don't ever want to go back, Beau."

"Come on Mel, just tell me what you saw."

Melissa slipped off the bench and sat on the ground. "When I travelled this time, it wasn't to the shrine but to some kind of filthy jail where Hippasus is being held. It was horrible. Just a pile of straw smeared with manure and a bowl of smelly water. His legs and arms were tied. They're treating him like a goat."

"We don't treat any of our goats like that."

"No, of course not. I can't believe they sacrificed human beings, a little boy!"

"Why do they want to kill Hippasus anyway?"

Melissa reached for the basket of bees, turned it upside down, and shook all the bees to the ground. "They blame him for a fever that's killed a lot of people."

Beau took the basket from Melissa and started to pick up bees.

"Don't bother, Beau."

"But there must be something we can do, some way to reverse his death sentence."

"Beau, we live twenty-six hundred years in his future. Face it, it's already happened. He's dead."

"Would your Mom know how to help?"

"Why would she? She doesn't know about my seizures. You're the only one I've told."

Beau took out his ball of clay and rolled it between his hands. "I just mean she might know about human sacrifice in Ancient Crete. If we knew more, maybe we could figure out a way to help him."

"You just don't get it, Beau." Melissa stood up and turned towards the porch steps. She looked over her shoulder and said, "Beau, go home. I want to be alone. Can't you leave me alone for once?"

"Mel—"

"I mean it. Just go. And don't bother to pick up any more bees."

"Mel, it's taken weeks to fold these."

"I never want to see an origami bee again."

"But what about your vow? The bees are for your father, right?"

Melissa glared at Beau. "Are you kidding, Beau? The real bees are gone and nothing's going to cheer up my father. Especially nothing I do."

Melissa stomped up the porch steps, entered the house and slammed the door. She'd seen the hurt look in Beau's face, but it was too late to take back her words.

When she was sure that Beau was gone, Melissa went outside and gathered up the bees, crumpling many of them in her hands. She tossed them, basket and all, into the compost bin. She slumped down on the porch steps and buried her face in her hands. Hermes nudged her with his cool nose as tears stained her cheeks.

She wanted to erase the past month from her mind, but how could she? She had shared something with Hippasus that felt extraordinary and real. And what about the Yolo bees? What was she supposed to do? Maybe Beau was right about her mother. But she couldn't tell her about the visions. Her mother would never believe any of it. Finally, Melissa rehearsed what to say before she tapped her holo-band.

It was late afternoon in Texas, close to midnight in Crete. She hoped it wasn't too late, but when a virtual image of Claire Berry rose into the air, she could see her mother was having dinner at some outdoor restaurant. Her mother's cheeks were slightly sunburned and she was holding a glass of wine in one hand. A platter piled with stuffed grape leaves was set on the table in front of her. Melissa was surprised to see Colin Anderson sitting nearby. What was he doing in Dia? Her mother had never mentioned he was going to be part of the dig team.

"Melissa?" her mother looked happily surprised. "I'm having a late dinner with colleagues."

"Oh, sorry. Should I call back later?"

"No, of course not, just let me move to a quieter spot. There. What's up?"

"I was thinking about that statuette you found."

"The young athlete? A gorgeous piece, isn't it? It made me think of you."

Melissa noticed the running shoe charm on the silver chain around her mother's neck and instinctively raised her hand to touch her own.

"So, have you found out if there was a race on Dia?"

Her mother shook her head of red curls and half-frowned. "No, I'm afraid not. We've sifted through several layers of the site and except for a few shards of broken vases and stones from a very old shrine, there's not been anything to confirm my theory yet."

"Nothing at all?"

Her mother shrugged. "Afraid not. I always knew it was a long shot." Claire Berry looked at her daughter and her eyes registered concern. "Are you alright, Melissa?"

"I'm fine, Mom. Hey, I was wondering, um, could that site have been used for human sacrifice?"

Her mother's eyebrows shot up. "Goodness, what made you think of that?"

"Well, didn't they sacrifice humans in ancient times?"

"Sometimes," her mother conceded, "but it was rare in the eras I study. Sometimes a community might try to purge itself of a plague or other misfortune by selecting a scapegoat, usually someone already accused of crimes and slated for execution."

Melissa fingered her racing shoe charm. "Would they kill someone just because he was different?"

"How do you mean?" Her mother looked puzzled.

"Well, if someone looked different, like if he had a hoof instead of a foot?"

"A hoof?"

Melissa realized how silly it must sound and quickly added, "You know, an infant born with a clubfoot or something."

"Infant exposure was certainly practiced. Fathers had the right to decide if a newborn lived or died. But why this sudden interest in human sacrifice?"

"It's just something I came across while reading and was wondering about. Did victims chosen for sacrifice ever get a reprieve?"

"A reprieve? Not that I know of unless they managed to escape." Her mother twirled the glass of wine in her hand then took a sip. She looked slightly distracted. She probably wanted to get back to dinner with Colin.

"Melissa, you seem a little agitated. Is something going on that I should know about?"

"No, everything's fine."

Her mother touched her running shoe charm. "I miss you, Honeybee. I miss our runs."

"I don't use that nickname anymore, Mom."

"Alright, but I do miss our runs."

"Me, too. I'm running a 5K on Sunday."

"Are you? That's great. Let's find a race to run together as soon as I can visit you in Texas."

"Sure, because Ba's never going to."

Her mother smiled. "No, he was never into running. Well, I should probably rejoin my colleagues."

"Okay, Mom. Bye."

"Bye, Melissa. I love you."

"Love you, too."

That evening, Melissa half-heartedly poked a pair of chopsticks into the bowl of fried rice she'd prepared for dinner. The usual pile of fruity and veggie pills sat by her plate next to a glass of water. Her father served himself a second bowl. He hadn't shown that much appetite in days.

"Ba, is the Yolo queen still alive?"

"Yes, and oddly enough, she and the remaining worker bees have calmed down. They even seem cheerful. They act as if they expect the other bees to return."

Surprised, Melissa sat up in her chair. "How do you tell if a honeybee is cheerful?" she asked.

"Part of my research has been to measure emotional response in honeybees. I'm pretty sure I can identify cheerful-ness, or at least a form of honeybee optimism."

Melissa realized there was a lot about her father's research she didn't know about. Another time, she'd have to ask him about honeybee emotions.

"Do you think the other bees might still return?"

"It's pretty doubtful. They've been gone for several days." He sounded resigned, but Melissa's spirits suddenly perked. Her father placed his bowl in the sink and retired to his study, leaving the dishes for Melissa. She washed them up in a hurry, grabbed a pack of origami paper then signaled Hermes to jog with her to Beau's. Rocio directed her to the goat shed where she found Beau sitting on a stool milking a goat.

"Beau, I'm really sorry about earlier."

He shrugged.

"I was upset."

He pointed to a corner of the shed. There sat the basket of bees she had thrown into the compost bin.

"Where? How did you?"

"I figured you might do something rash. I didn't want you to regret it later."

Melissa didn't know whether to be angry that he'd spied on her or grateful. She sat down beside him to watch him milk Pandora. The goat munched contentedly on some kind of pellets while Beau squeezed her milk into a silver bucket. As the milk splashed against the metal sides of the pail, it made a pleasant sound like the shaking of hand bells.

"Those alfalfa pellets she's eating, they're worth their weight in gold," he said.

"Aren't there milking machines to do that work?"

"Sure, but sometimes it's nicer to do things the old way."

"Is that hard to do?"

"Not once you get the hang of it. Here, let me show you." Beau stood up from the stool and gestured for Melissa to sit on it instead. He crouched behind her and placed his hands over hers, showing her how to grasp the teat with her thumb and forefinger and then squeeze with the rest of her fingers in a smooth, successive motion. Melissa found the firm, confident touch of Beau's hands around her own comforting.

"Ba says the Yolo queen is acting optimistic. I'm going to try to travel again, Beau. I'm scared but I know I have to do it."

"Right now?"

"Right now. You in?"

"You bet. This is the last goat I have to milk. We can wash our hands and be off. Back to the lavender field?"

Melissa shook her head. "No, I thought to the riverbank. They want to drown Hippasus and I'm thinking being near water might help."

"Okay. And I can show you where the trail for Sunday's 5K starts."

Amethea felt battered by waves of fear, anger, and remorse. She could not quiet her mind. Hippasus was sentenced to drown at high tide in two days, bound and tethered like a goat to a wooden post in the sea. A scapegoat, a sacrifice to cleanse the island and appease the gods. She had condemned her own brother by her cowardice; had placed winning a race above his life. Her tears fell as she placed wild poppies and daisies on the shrine altar. In her other hand she clutched the gold votive figure of the goddess. She pressed it to her breast before placing it in the center of the flowers then lay down on the cracked marble floor. The broken tiles were like a scattering of bones.

A waning gibbous moon, white as a bowl of milk, spilled light over the shrine. She searched for the blue heart of the lion and found it; but it brought no comfort to her own bruised heart. Dove had followed her to the shrine and tried to comfort her by licking her tear-stained face.

"I do not deserve your pity, Dove." She looked into the hound's amber, almond-shaped eyes. "When the elders came for Hippasus, you growled and would have protected him with your sharp teeth, but I held you back." She buried her face in Dove's soft blond fur and wept.

She thought back to that scene, how the elders had first spoken to Hippasus in sweet voices, saying they intended to escort him to a banquet in his honor. Hippasus did not believe them and tried to hobble away. One man caught him and the other placed a rope around his neck.

"If you won't come willingly, we'll drag you, son of a goat," the man snarled.

Hippasus had implored Amethea with his eyes, but she stood by impassively.

"Go with them, brother." Karpos had told her she must steel her heart.

"Thanks to Karpos," the man who held the rope said, "we have a sacrifice to end the fever."

Amethea looked at him, stunned. "It was my uncle's idea, not orders of the Council?"

"Only a man as sure of himself as your uncle would have suggested a human sacrifice. That took some guts," said the other man.

Amethea felt sickened as she watched them lead Hippasus away. Her uncle had lied to her, betrayed his own kin.

Now as she lay on the cold stones in the shrine, she cried, "Artemis, Goddess of Bees, tell me what I must do to save my brother! Send me a dream!"

An hour passed, then two. The moon slid across the sky. Amethea lay as if paralyzed, too miserable to fall asleep. Finally, she sat up and hugged her knees to her chest, then reached for the woolen shawl wrapped around her aulos. She placed the flutes in her mouth and played a mournful tune, lifting her fingers up and down over the holes. An owl, white as sea foam, passed overhead on silent wings and for an instant blotted out moon and stars.

Amethea put her flutes down and crawled to a corner of the shrine where Hippasus kept his pebbles. He had made a counting sequence with them, placing one pebble, then two, then three, all the way to ten pebbles arranged in a tidy triangle. He had lined up other pebbles to create geometric figures including several hexagons linked together like a honeycomb. Hippasus had told her that the pebbles were helping him to learn the language of honeybees. She placed her palm over the pebbles now and softly counted from one to ten. What had Hippasus meant? Did honeybees speak in numbers and shapes?

"Goat boy! Goat boy!" the village boys had taunted Hippasus, and the uncouth tanner made hand gestures to ward off evil when he saw her brother. But prior to the fever, no one ever suggested he deserved death. The fever had poisoned their minds. Rich and influential Karpos had darkened their minds even more. She now knew it was Karpos himself who insisted on a sacrifice and had offered his own nephew, pretending it was a noble, selfless act, when what he really wanted was to rid himself of any duty to the boy. Amethea wanted desperately to take back her agreement with him. She should have fled with Hippasus, but where? And now it was too late, too late.

As Amethea cupped her hand over the pebbles, she felt a sudden warm pulse rise from them. Startled, she lifted her hand. A small light flickered on and off over the pebbles. Was it some kind of insect, a firefly? No, it looked like a honeybee. Several other bees popped in and out of sight, each like a tiny burning lamp. One dropped lifeless among the pebbles. Amethea stared at it and then nudged it with her finger. She gasped when the body of the bee unfolded itself into a small square. She lifted the square and peered at it. It was made of the same material as the ornament bee her brother had shown her, the one that had flown into the tree snag to join the shrine bees. The square folded itself back into a plump bee and flew to the altar stone where the gold votive of the bee goddess began to softly glow. An image of a dark-haired girl running flashed across her mind as it had once before. The Bee Maker was sending her a message!

Amethea knew what she must do.

CHAPTER FIFTEEN

PYTHAGORAS OF SAMOS

At sunrise, Amethea left the shrine. She draped her shawl over her head and shoulders and carried a laurel branch, the sign of a supplicant, as she made her way to the home of her friend Kleis. Kleis' father sat on the Council and her mother had been a trusted friend of Amethea's mother. Amethea hurried over the stony path until she reached a house with a clay-tiled roof, three times the size of her own cottage. The mud brick walls were painted in swirls of blue and green.

She entered the courtyard and was met by a slave girl with thin arms and a sullen expression. When the girl returned with Kleis' mother, Amethea was shocked to see how drawn and pale her face was. Her eyes were ringed with dark shadows and patches of her golden hair had been yanked out, a sign of mourning. With a stiff nod she acknowledged Amethea but did not invite her to sit. Her mantle was torn; strips of cloth hung like limp snakes as if she wore a version of Medusa's severed head as a breastplate of sorrow. Or rage.

A wall of doubt closed around Amethea. Someone had died in the household. The woman stared at her with vacant, accusing eyes. Amethea barely managed a whisper when she spoke. "As a sister-friend to Kleis and in remembrance of your friendship with my mother, I come as a supplicant to speak with your husband."

"Dead, both dead," the woman said in a clipped monotone.

"Kleis, dead?" Amethea's voice trembled.

"Kleis. My husband. The fever stole them both in the night."

"Oh, no!" Amethea cried, "I loved Kleis."

"Why are you here?" the woman demanded.

"I came to beseech your husband's help for my condemned brother."

The woman spat on the stones before Amethea's feet. "There is not a person on Dia who would spare the monster Hippasus."

"Hippasus cannot be blamed for the fever," Amethea protested. "Our own mother is dead."

"Leave! and take your polluted words with you." Kleis' mother turned abruptly and disappeared through the door of her house. The slave girl scowled at Amethea before following on the heels of her mistress.

Her eyes stinging with tears, Amethea stumbled over narrow goat trails. She couldn't bear to return to the cottage where wilted celery boughs hung in the house like ghosts. At last she turned her steps in the direction of the village market, her shawl drawn over her face so only her eyes showed. She slipped between vendor stalls where merchants hawked clay pots, jars of goat cheese, and packets of purple dye ground from seashells.

The bustle of life continued despite the fever, despite the death of Kleis, despite the fate that awaited Hippasus.

She glanced up and spotted Dika at the far end of the square where she was busy scooping up sesame seeds with an olivewood ladle. Amethea turned away and saw a crowd gathering near the market center. There a Dia elder, perched on a block of marble, began to address the crowd. She stifled a gasp when she saw Hippasus behind him, his neck and hands bound with ropes.

"This son of a goat will be sacrificed tomorrow morning at high tide. He will perish in the sea and take the fever with him."

Shouts of approval went up from the crowd. Amethea pressed her body against the side of a shop and stared in horror. Two hollow goat horns had been tied over the stubs on his head and he was naked. She wanted to rush to him and take his thin, frightened body into her arms, but the elder yanked at the ropes that bound him and shoved him back towards the jailhouse.

Two men stood near an herbalist's shop opposite Amethea and watched the scene with solemn faces. The older man, obviously a foreigner, was dressed in a pair of white linen trousers and a white over-tunic that reached to his knees. His jet-black hair fell past his shoulders in thick curls. He had a hawk-like nose, a broad forehead and high cheekbones, a trimmed beard. She was struck by the intense gaze of his dark eyes, like burning coals or orbs of polished obsidian. The younger man had wheat-colored hair and was dressed in the usual chiton. He had an amiable, intelligent face, and a large papyrus scroll tucked under his left arm. Amethea had never seen them before.

Suddenly the market scene blurred before her eyes. She leaned against the shop wall as darkness swallowed her. When she came to it was to the scent of spices. The man in the white linen tunic was massaging her hands with aromatic oil poured from a small glass vial.

Dika crouched by her, moaning and wringing her hands. "Not the fever, please not the fever."

"There is no sign of fever," the man reassured her. "Her skin is cool, but she has suffered a shock."

"Seeing her brother tethered like a goat," Dika muttered.

People who had gathered to listen to the elder's proclamation had dispersed and there was no sign of Hippasus. Amethea tried to sit up but another wave of dizziness prevented her.

The man in white motioned for her to lie still, then turned to Dika and said, "Is the dwelling of your mistress close by? She is not strong enough to walk on her own, but my companion and I will be glad to support her steps."

Dika waivered and the older man read her reluctance.

"My name is Pythagoras," he said. "Pythagoras of Samos. I journey with Hecataeus of Miletus. We are men of honor. I serve Apollo through the study of Number and Music. We are headed for Croton, but at my insistence, our ship has anchored in Dia. I came seeking some of your island's legendary honey. I never expected to find human sacrifice here."

Dika appeared dumbfounded by this unexpected and lengthy speech, but its effect on Amethea was like a splash of cold water. She sat upright and clasped the august man's hand.

"Hippasus studies Number! His pebbles make pictures before the altar of the Bee Goddess. I can lead you to the finest source of honey on the island, but you must agree to help my brother!"

It was Pythagoras' turn to look startled and he peered at Amethea with a hard gaze as if gauging whether or not she was infected with fever or madness or both. But then his gaze softened and he motioned to his friend to help her to her feet. Hecataeus placed an arm around her waist to provide support but she lightly pushed it away.

"I feel better now. The clouds have cleared from my head."

"Your brother is the young goat boy, the sacrificial victim," murmured Pythagoras.

Amethea nodded. "We should not speak here," she said, "but if you will come with me, I will take you to the shrine of the Bee Goddess and show you my brother's counting pebbles." She led the two men up the narrow, rocky trails until they reached the secret shrine hidden among thorny acanthus and wild thyme bushes. There she dipped a wooden spoon into a small clay urn and scooped out a piece of honeycomb dripping with honey. She handed it to Pythagoras and he closed his eyes as he tasted the honey. He stood without moving for so long that Amethea wondered if he, like Hippasus, had spells. She felt herself grow calm. Serenity emanated from the philosopher as if he possessed an invisible power that could gather every natural sound, bird trill and bee drone, crashing wave and soughing wind, into one unified song.

At last he opened his eyes and spoke. "This is honey blessed. Dia is indeed touched by the Goddess."

"Hippasus, my brother, gathered this honey." She pointed to the tree snag that housed the hive. "The bees allow him to take honey from time to time, as though they consider him kin. They do not sting or chase him as they would anyone else."

Pythagoras gazed out over the cliff at the restless sea. He turned to Hecataeus and said, "As I had hoped, honey from Dia will be a worthy gift to offer the priests in Hyperborea." His companion nodded.

Amethea looked puzzled. "Hyperborea? Where is that?."

"Farther than any man from Samos or Miletus or Crete has ever been," the younger man with wheat-colored hair answered.

"How will you find it if no one has ever been there?"

"Apollo has shown me in dreams," said Pythagoras, "and I travel with the most learned geographer in all the world." He nodded at Hecataeus who sat on a flat rock twirling a twig of thyme in his mouth. The geographer's eyes danced and Amethea found it hard to believe that a man who looked barely past thirty could be so learned.

"What is a geographer?" she asked.

Hecataeus answered, "One who travels by foot and by sea to known and unknown places. From my travels, I have drawn a map that shows the farthest known boundaries of the world. Hyperborea lies yet beyond."

"Before you travel there, will you help my brother?"

"Show me your brother's pebbles," said Pythagoras.

Amethea pointed to the ground behind the altar stone. Pythagoras examined the neat formations Hippasus had laid out. He knelt down and touched the one pebble, two pebbles, three pebbles, all the way to the triangle-shaped decad. He stroked the geometric figures Hippasus had made and measured some of them with a short rod he pulled from his tunic. He whispered syllables in a language Amethea had never heard, some kind of incantation, and traced Hippasus' hexagons several times with his forefinger. At last he stood up and Amethea was surprised to see tears glistening in his eyes.

He further surprised her by solemnly lifting his tunic and folding up his pant's leg to reveal his right thigh. She stared at it, awe-stricken, for his thigh, unlike the rest of his dark olive skin, was a bright golden color and covered in downy golden hairs like the fuzz on a honeybee. He looked into Amethea's wondering eyes and said, "Your brother has been marked by the gods, as have I." He folded his trouser leg back down.

"Tell me about your brother. What signs were there at his birth?"

Amethea told Pythagoras how a swarm of honeybees had hovered in the doorway to welcome Hippasus when he was born and how their father, repulsed by his infant son's deformed foot and head bumps had abandoned the family. "My mother held Hippasus in her arms and would not relinquish him. My father had brought daffodils and violets to honor my mother but threw them down in disgust when he saw Hippasus. But the bees, they hovered near Hippasus for days as if they meant to protect him."

"What is this? It looks like a honeybee." Pythagoras lifted something from the altar and held it aloft in his palm.

"Hippasus said that came from the Bee Maker."

"The Bee Maker? Tell me more, child."

"Hippasus has spells. He grows still and looks into the air and sees things others do not. Shortly after our mother died, he said that the Bee Maker came and gave him that ornament."

Hecataeus who had been listening quietly leaned forward, his eyes round with interest.

Pythagoras examined the origami bee closely, touching every surface and angle of it with his fingertip. "What strange and marvelous material, so light and thin. It is not skin or linen or hammered gold or any leaf I know of. Who is this Bee Maker? A priestess on your island?"

"I have never seen her, Sir. Only Hippasus sees her when he is in a spell. Hippasus thinks she is in the service of Artemis, or even Artemis herself."

"This is a marvel of craftsmanship. I should like to learn how it was made."

"At first I thought my brother had somehow made it himself, but I couldn't guess how. Sometimes it moves, comes to life. It unfolds into a square and then back into a bee."

Pythagoras blew softly on the origami bee. In a low voice, he sang again in a foreign tongue and moved his legs and arms in a slow, flowing dance as he held the origami bee aloft. The ornament bee remained an ornament, but that did not seem to bother Pythagoras. He stroked the body and wings and dangling legs. Amethea could tell he was fascinated and wanted to know how it was made.

"Forgive me, Bee Maker," he whispered, as he slowly and gently unfolded the origami bee until he held a small square of paper. He studied the square and with his finger traced triangles and angles formed by fold lines in the paper. "Amethea, with your consent, I would like to examine this ornament further. It has much to teach me."

Amethea nodded and Pythagoras tucked the paper square into his tunic.

"Will you help my brother?" Amethea asked again, her voice urgent.

"I dreamt I would find my greatest pupil on Dia. I have found him."

Pythagoras turned to Hecataeus and said, "We must find a way to ransom the boy's life and then take him with us to Hyperborea." He turned to Amethea. "With your consent, I will care for Hippasus as my own son."

Relief rippled through Amethea's limbs. "Will you ask the Council elders to release him to you?"

Pythagoras shook his head. "Your elders have already issued a proclamation. Pride will not allow them to retract it. I must think on this. Can we return to your home?"

"We have little time," said Amethea. "They mean to drown him tomorrow morning."

"If he is under the protection of the Bee Maker, we will find a way."

Back at the cottage, Amethea prepared a simple meal of wild leeks simmered with purslane and served it to her guests with a small round of goat cheese. They tore sections from a flat loaf of barley bread and dipped the crusts in olive oil. She apologized she had no meat to serve such illustrious guests but Pythagoras informed her he abstained from meat.

"Hippasus has made the same vow!"

"Meat dulls the mind," Pythagoras said, "and Apollo abhors blood sacrifice. Upon his altar only honey, wildflowers, and branches of laurel should be offered."

Amethea pondered his words, she who had always hoped to win the victor's share of the slaughtered ox at the Heraea Games. She caught the glance of Hecataeus who stood behind Pythagoras. He lifted an eyebrow. He, she sensed, would not refuse onions grilled with lamb or a spiced blood sausage.

Refreshed by food, Pythagoras plied Amethea with questions. When he learned she was a runner and that her uncle Karpos had persuaded her to accept her brother's sacrifice by promising to escort her to the Heraea Games that summer, he clapped his hands together and said, "That is it, that is how I will approach your Dia elders."

"What do you mean?" asked Amethea.

"In distant times," Pythagoras explained, "when human sacrifice was more common than it is now, I have heard that the victim was sometimes offered a chance to escape. The gods admire athletic talent as much as burnt offerings and a swift runner might thus secure his freedom. I will appeal to your elders to allow for this chance."

"But Hippasus cannot run!" protested Amethea. "You have seen his foot. He could never outrun anyone."

"I do not speak of your goat-footed brother," Pythagoras said, and somehow the way he said the epithet 'goat-footed' did not sound insulting but affectionate. "I speak of you."

Amethea stared at him, not understanding.

"Amethea, refuse the Heraea Games and ask instead to run a race here on Dia to save your brother. If you win your race, Hippasus goes free. I will leave at once and seek an audience with the Council to persuade them to accept this."

With his impressive height, piercing eyes, and learned speech, Pythagoras was a formidable figure, but Amethea wondered, would the Council heed a stranger? After he had left, Hecataeus assured her that Pythagoras was known and esteemed by eminent priests and powerful kings throughout Babylonia, Egypt, and Greece. "If any man can sway your elders, it is Pythagoras."

"What did he mean, Hecataeus, when he said he had found a pupil here?"

"After our voyage to Hyperborea, Pythagoras plans to start a school in Croton. He will teach initiates the secrets of Number and Music. Hippasus, he believes, will become his greatest student."

"How can he know this?"

"Pythagoras speaks with Apollo."

"Like Hippasus speaks with the Bee Goddess."

"Artemis," observed the geographer, "is Apollo's twin sister."

Amethea nodded, but her stomach twisted with fear and worry as she anxiously awaited Pythagoras' return. It was mid-afternoon when she finally heard his firm, sure steps coming up the path. She ran to greet him and hurriedly led him into the cottage where she poured him a cup of wine.

She held her breath, waiting for him to speak. Hecataeus leaned forward, anxious to learn the Council's decision.

"It is decided," said Pythagoras. "Amethea, you will be given a chance to race for your brother's life tomorrow morning. However," he paused as if reluctant to share the conditions, "you must race against the swiftest boy your age on Dia."

Hecataeus exclaimed, "A maiden to race against a young man? Do they think she is Atalanta? This is no way to give Hippasus a chance."

"They do not want to give him a chance," said Amethea.

"That is not all," said Pythagoras. "The elders have decided the race will be a dolichos."

"This is madness!" shouted Hecataeus.

Amethea was stunned. The dolichos, run by male athletes at the Olympics, was twenty-four stades long. At the Heraea Games, the women's footrace was a mere stade, a couple hundred meters. She straightened her shoulders and bowed to Pythagoras.

"You have done your best."

"This is the only way the elders will allow Hippasus a chance to be spared." His eyes were full of kindness but also the harder edge of challenge.

"Eucles," she murmured. "They mean Eucles. He is the youth chosen to carry messages from one end of the island to the other on account of his swift feet. I have seen him run along the shore calling to dolphins as if they were his kin. I could never beat him in a race, especially one so long."

"Would you refuse to try?" Pythagoras asked.

She looked down at her sandaled feet. How could they ever bear her fast enough to beat Eucles over such a long distance? Yet, how could she refuse? "No," she said, "I do not refuse. I will race this dolichos."

"Your spirit is strong, child. Eucles may run as a dolphin swims, but you will run as swift as the fiery horse you are named for. The race will begin on the beach and wind up and over the island before returning to the start line. The trail is to be marked by red ribbons. The council is already sending out men to measure and mark the trail." He paused, then added, "Your uncle Karpos argued against this race but when he could not prevail, he is the one who insisted it be a dolichos."

Amethea rose and walked to the trellis of white roses. It was covered with new blooms. "I will offer flowers on the altar of the Bee Goddess and pray for her help." She walked with graceful, firm steps, but inside she already felt defeated.

CHAPTER SIXTEEN

ATTACK

As Amethea made her way to the shrine with an armful of white roses, she suddenly stopped to listen. Someone was following her; the sound of hasty footsteps and labored breathing could only belong to Karpos. Fearful, she looked behind and there he was, gaining on her, red-faced and scowling. She tried to run but the hem of her tunic caught on a thorn and gave Karpos the extra moment he needed to reach her. He grabbed her arm and forced her around. Sneering, he dropped his hand but moved to block the path that led to the shrine. She glared at him.

"Let me pass, Uncle."

"Niece, why this sudden coldness?"

"There is nothing to say to each other."

"I know it is hard for you to accept your brother's death, but you are an athlete. You must show courage."

"I will summon my courage when I race against Eucles."

Amethea tried to walk around Karpos but he shoved her back in place and gripped her arm. She flung her head, shaking a tumble of red curls.

"You would defy the gods? This is folly, Amethea. You cannot hope to win. You will destroy your only chance to claim true victory at Olympia."

"I was blind to accept your offer. Hippasus' life means more to me than the Heraea Games."

"You would throw away your dream, you who could be Atalanta and bring glory to Crete?"

Amethea knew it was hopeless to race against Eucles. She could never hope to outrun him, but at least Hippasus would drown knowing she had not abandoned him, had not placed the Heraea Games above his life. Her eyes flashed defiance. "If you are so certain I cannot win this race, why bother trying to dissuade me? You will have what you want in the end."

Karpos tensed his jaw and Amethea was surprised to detect uncertainty beneath his hard gaze. He was not completely convinced she would lose!

"Amethea, do not disgrace our family by running this race." His grip on her arm tightened and she cried out in pain.

"There is nothing you can say that will change my mind."

"Nothing I can say? But there is plenty I can do."

She struggled to break away from his hold but he seized her with both arms and shoved his face against hers. He snarled, "You are a fool, niece."

He pushed her to the ground and straddled her body with his thick legs, his face a mask of rage. He scooped a rock from the ground and raised his arm in a threatening gesture. She screamed and to her surprise, he dropped the rock and looked wildly about him. Something strange was happening to the air.

A frenzied blur of gold and black took shape and clamped over Karpos' head like a writhing helmet. He yelled and began to slap at his own face and chest. Like a man possessed, he batted at the air as it filled with hundreds of gold arrows. The bees! In fury, they attacked Karpos. He scrambled to his feet and hurdled down the path pursued by an army of enraged bees.

At that moment, Hecataeus came running from the direction of the cottage followed by a barking Dove. Seeing the geographer, Amethea grabbed her shawl and flung it over her bruised body. She tried to stand but fell back down with a cry.

"I heard you scream," Hecataeus gasped, nearly out of breath. "By the gods, what has happened?"

"Karpos."

His eyes flashed in anger and he turned to pursue her attacker but Amethea lifted a hand and said, "No, let him go. It is over."

Concern tempered the anger in the geographer's eyes as he knelt down to assist her. "Amethea, are you hurt? Did he—"

"No," she answered, "Artemis sent her bees. But my ankle—" She gritted her teeth against the rising pain. Her left ankle was gashed and bleeding, dark as a mash of grapes and rapidly swelling. She had twisted it beneath her and dashed it against a sharp rock when Karpos flung her to the ground.

At that moment all hope died in Amethea's breast. "I cannot run now. I cannot run." Tears streamed down her face. The ground where she sat was littered with the bodies of dying bees that had sacrificed themselves to protect her. Artemis, the Bee Goddess, had sent her sacred, brave messengers, but Karpos had still won. There was no chance to save Hippasus now. Amethea lifted a dead bee in her hand, bowed her head over it and wept bitterly. Hecataeus' face filled with sorrow as he gazed at the red-haired young woman bereft of hope. He lifted her in his arms and carried her back to the cottage, stepping over tattered white roses and dead bees.

Melissa and Beau biked to the riverbank with Hermes riding in his basket. When they arrived, Beau led them to the spot where the next morning's 5K would start. They leaned their bikes against a towering cypress and sat beneath it. Melissa kicked off her shoes. Dozens of knobby cypress knees thrust up along the riverbank like troops of miniature dwarves. Watercress with small white flowers floated at the water's edge close to the trail. A massive pecan tree with flaked red bark stood close by. These were survivor trees and sitting beneath them strengthened Melissa's resolve.

She took two pieces of origami paper from her pack, handed one to Beau, and they both began folding. After several minutes, she completed one bee and proceeded to fold a second, doing her best to conjure an image of Hippasus in her mind, imagining him not as she had last seen him, tethered to a rope in the jail cell, but how he had looked the day he brought the Yolo bees to the lavender field. They had surrounded him like the rings of Saturn. She tried to relax her mind, remembering how Noi had said surrender could be a path to joy. She hoped it was also a path to connecting with Hippasus and to calling the Yolo bees home.

It began. She heard the strains of flute music and felt the rise of nameless panic, a tingling in her limbs coupled with fear she might dissolve, blank out permanently, never find her way home. She gave herself to it anyway.

"Mel?" Beau looked up from his own folding and saw Melissa staring straight ahead. He understood she was travelling, but then to his utter surprise, watched as a golden light rippled down her arms and across her face. Her hair sparkled with tiny red fires and her skin glowed like the translucent surface of a pearl. Her entire body glowed, shimmered, faded in and out of sight. Then to Beau's great alarm, Melissa vanished. Hermes, who had been lying beside her, lifted his head and howled.

Melissa, shocked and helpless, witnessed Karpos attack Amethea. She saw the honeybees come to Amethea's aid and the arrival of Hecataeus. She now followed the geographer as he carried Amethea back to the cottage. As she picked her feet over thorns and stones, she could sense the physical movements of her body but when she looked down at her feet or lifted her hands in front of her eyes, all she could see was a fading gold light, and then even that disappeared. Was she still sitting beneath the cypress tree and only her mind had travelled? Yes, that's how it had been before. The seizures had caused hallucinations. But why then did she feel so present, so *physically* present right now?

She could feel the weight of her body and her heart pounding in her chest. The soles of her feet felt the soft grasses and sharp stones. She even felt a lock of her hair fall over one eye. And though she could not see even one particle of her body, she knew with every fiber of her being that she was more present in the world of Amethea and Hippasus than she had ever been before. What she felt was not the thin, hypnotic quality of her other seizures, but a bracing, raw sense of being bodily in the here and now of Ancient Dia. Her invisible arms prickled with invisible goose bumps. Was she invisible because the particles that made up her body were not cohering? How had Bella explained that property of quarks? And what if all the billions of quarks that made Melissa *Melissa* suddenly blinked out of existence entirely?

Melissa fought a wave of terror and nausea. She tried to convince herself that Beau was still with her, that he was sitting beside her beneath the cypress tree waiting for her to snap out of a seizure. But could her body be in two places at once? She steeled herself. Whatever was happening, she had work to do here. Though how she might save Hippasus or retrieve the Yolo bees, she had no clue. She continued to follow Hecataeus back to the cottage, desperate for some sign. She slipped in the doorway and watched as he placed Amethea on a low couch. Dika, shouting curses against Karpos, rushed about gathering strips of wool. She told Hecataeus that Pythagoras had left for the village shortly beforehand, saying he wanted to walk along the shore there.

"He was holding a small square of something," she said. "Kept folding it this way and that."

Dika crushed several cloves of garlic and mixed the pulp with wine vinegar, which she applied as a poultice over Amethea's ankle. She then wrapped the ankle in strips of clean wool. Assured that Dika could best tend to Amethea's injury, Hecataeus went off to find Pythagoras. Dove curled at the foot of the couch and softly whined.

"Do not despair, Amethea," Hecataeus said before departing. "Pythagoras will not allow your brother to drown. Nor will I."

Pythagoras? Did he mean the famous mathematician, Melissa wondered.

Dika gave Amethea a strong draught of wine mixed with herbs to ease the pain and help her sleep. Amethea turned her face to the wall. She could still feel the brutal press of Karpos' hands on her body. She felt unclean and defeated as she fell into a troubled sleep.

Melissa continued to watch, befuddled by a body that was both there and not there. She tried to remember what Bella had said the evening they first met, something about how bees might use quarks to coil messages inside other dimensions. Was she herself coiled within other dimensions that couldn't be seen in the three dimensional space of Dia? The creeping fear that she would dissolve into nothingness gripped her. Bella had said something about gluons, too, sticky particles that held matter together. Had Melissa come un-glued?

The afternoon slipped into violet dusk then darkened to indigo night. Melissa lowered her non-body beside Amethea's couch to rest. She longed to find herself back beneath the cypress tree along the banks of the Sabinal River, next to Beau and Hermes. Would she ever get home? Sometime past midnight, with a waning moon shining through the doorway and casting a soft glow over Amethea, Melissa saw a thin golden light begin to outline her own body. She felt a tingling in her arms and legs as the light revealed her body's contours. What happened next she could never fully describe but she felt a stretching and thinning of her body as if she were being divided into many small parts, separate and yet connected. She transformed into a long, undulating line of honeybees that contracted into a swarm and then stretched back out into a line. This line spiraled around and around Amethea until it formed a diaphanous cloud. All the particles of Melissa moved with the collective mind of a honeybee swarm and in that form hovered over Amethea, humming the songs she had heard Amethea play on the aulos. And Melissa suddenly understood what it is that mystics feel.

An hour before sunrise, Amethea awoke to find Pythagoras sitting beside her intoning a healing chant and moving his cupped hands over her ankle. He had removed the strips of wool bandage. Hecataeus and an anxious Dika stood behind him. The swelling and discoloration had disappeared. There was no sign of gash or sprain. At Pythagoras' bidding Amethea sat up and placed her foot gingerly on the floor. She slowly stood and placed weight on the foot. She felt a few pricks of pain but they eased as she took a few steps. Encouraged, she walked around the room.

"I am healed!" she cried. She jogged around the room, her laughter rising like the babble of a creek. She pranced about like a spirited horse. There remained a mild ache and stiffness in her ankle but that was nothing. "Blessed are Dika's herbs and the invocations of Pythagoras!" She flung her arms into the air.

"More than that, I think," said Pythagoras as he handed her an origami bee. When I arrived last night, I found this perched on your ankle."

"Ornament of the Bee Maker!" marveled Amethea. "Artemis has been here in the night." She lifted her foot. "My ankle is as lithe as a nymph's. I will run my race, after all!"

Dove came bounding in from the courtyard.

"She slept beside the couch all night," said Hecataeus, "and would not leave your side."

Amethea bent down and kissed the top of the dog's blond head. Dove leapt about the girl and barked with joy.

"There is no time to lose," warned Pythagoras. "Preparations for the sacrifice will already have begun. Bathe and put on your race chiton, Amethea." He turned to Hecataeus, "Hurry to town and inform the Dia elders that the race will proceed. I am sure Karpos has told them otherwise."

Hecataeus was off like an arrow from Apollo's bow.

In her mother's chamber, Amethea undressed. She smoothed scented olive oil over her skin and with Dika's help scraped it off with a strigil, a curved metal tool used to clean the body. Dika handed her the race chiton that Amethea's mother had so lovingly embroidered. With a gold brooch, she joined two ends of the cloth over Amethea's left breast and shoulder, but left Amethea's right breast bare in the manner prescribed for races. The chiton fell just above her knees. This, Amethea thought, is how Atalanta dressed when she raced her doomed suitors.

Amethea strapped on her sandals and hastened down the path towards the village. A crowd had gathered and the air pulsed like lyre strings too tightly strung. Some spectators parted to let her pass. When others tried to block her way, she pushed her way through. The mother of Kleis, wearing a dark veil of mourning, turned away as if to shun her. Vendors snaked through the crowd hawking thorn-covered branches and crude-shaped toys made of clay. Amethea saw with disgust that the toys were meant to represent Hippasus, grotesque shapes of a half-boy half-goat. Several people were slashing the clay toy with thorns to purge their grief and anger over loved ones lost to the fever.

Amethea halted when she reached the strip of beach where the race would begin. Farther down the shore, a wooden pedestal had been erected on which two elders stood, one a stout man with a blond beard and an air of self-importance, the other tall and angular with a pinched expression on his face. They took turns addressing the crowd, telling them that the sacrifice would soon cleanse the island of fever. The clamor of the crowd surged and then fell to an uneasy silence as people parted to let the guard pass who was charged with leading Hippasus into the sea.

Angry tears filled Amethea's eyes. Hippasus' hands were tightly bound and another rope was looped around his neck. He struggled to hobble forward. The guard yanked impatiently at the rope and Hippasus tumbled face forward, gashing his lip on a stone. Some in the crowd jeered as blood trickled down his chin. Others whipped him with branches until his skin was raw and bleeding. Amethea forced her way to him and helped him stand back up. He lifted his head and smiled weakly at her. Through cracked and bleeding lips, he whispered, "Amethea, will you run? Karpos said you would not."

"Karpos is a liar."

"Amethea, I wish I could hear you tell the story of Atalanta one last time."

The guard jerked the rope around Hippasus' neck again and snarled at Amethea. "Move aside."

"There is no need to tell a story, brother. I will be the story today."

"With the same ending?"

"There are no golden apples this time."

The guard shoved Hippasus forward as sister and brother shared a last glance.

The race had been timed to coincide with the creeping rise of the morning's tide. Early sunlight sparkled on the waves beneath a pale cloudless sky tinged rose at the edges. In the distance, a faint outline of the main island of Crete was visible.

The burly guard led Hippasus out into the waves until the water reached the boy's waist. Amethea watched as another man, one who sat on the Council, pounded a stake into the firm sand beneath the water's surface and then lashed Hippasus to it. When high tide crested, the water would cover his head and he would drown.

Already the water was beginning its slow creep. White-tipped waves lapped with a little more force as each minute passed. It was time for the race to begin. Not only did Amethea need to win it to ransom her brother's life, she needed to complete the course faster than the tides could rise. She looked over and saw Eucles adjusting his sandal. He wore only a narrow loincloth and a thin white headband. His body gleamed as if he had polished it. His legs were long and lean; he sported no beard yet, only a tumble of brown hair that grazed his shoulders.

Amethea jogged to the starting line and took her place beside him. Eucles stole a sideways glance at her and for an instant their eyes locked. He jerked his head ever so slightly and in that quick gesture, Amethea understood that he did not want to run this race. Was it because he was ashamed to race a girl? She did not know him well but he had always struck her as kind and cheerful. She liked how he called to the dolphins as he ran along the shore. Perhaps, she thought, he even felt pity for Hippasus.

Pythagoras and Hecataeus, she saw, stood impassively by the wooden platform where the race would end. Dika and Kimon, ever loyal, stood beside the two learned men. Dove, restrained by a rope leash, crouched beside the couple. Dika placed one hand on the hound's head to calm her. Her other hand clutched a votive figure of Pan. Kimon bent his head over something he held in his hands. Was he working with clay? How strange, Amethea thought, that he would be fashioning one of his little figures at such a moment.

Karpos strode forward, his face and upper body covered with welts. He avoided Amethea's eyes as he barked an order for the two runners to get ready. Amethea took a deep breath and before crouching behind the red ribbon, whispered, "Goddess, grant me swift feet." The last thing she noticed before the red ribbon dropped was the tiny, lone figure of Hippasus in the distance, half submerged in the salty waves. The seawater was heartbreakingly beautiful that morning, like pale blue glass shattered into shards.

CHAPTER SEVENTEEN

THE FIRE
OF CREATION

Beau bent down and did his best to comfort Hermes, though his own nerves were a mess. For an hour, he had searched up and down the riverbanks and trails for Melissa, franticly calling her name. Hermes refused to budge from the spot beneath the cypress tree where Melissa had last been.

"She's not here," Beau repeated to the dog. "I've looked everywhere." He resigned himself to the heavy task of finding Melissa's father and trying to explain what had happened. He knew that Dr. Bùi would find his story unbelievable. In a gamble for more time, he tapped his wristband and called his mother. The holo-screen showed her sitting at her loom.

"Beau? I thought you and Melissa would be back by now. You missed dinner and haven't answered your wristband."

"Sorry, Mom, we went for a walk down by the river and lost track of time. Uh, Mom, do you think it'd be all right if Melissa and I stayed out later, maybe caught a movie at the Student Union? There's a double feature tonight, science fiction flicks."

"It's alright with me, mijo, if her father agrees."

"Okay, Mom. Don't expect me back till late."

"Bueno, but doesn't Melissa have that race in the morning? Are you sure staying out late is a good idea?"

"Don't worry, Melissa's a monster. She says she actually races better on less sleep," he improvised.

Beau contacted Melissa's father next, striding several yards from the cypress tree where Hermes sat. He worried a few alarmed yips from the dog might signal something was amiss. When Paul Bùi appeared on the screen, Beau took a steadying breath. It was bad enough to fudge on the truth with his mother, but now he had to do the same with Melissa's father.

"Hey, Dr. Bùi, would it be okay if Melissa and I went to the movies on campus tonight?"

"Sure, Beau. You know you're welcome to call me Paul."

"I know, sir, but I like the sound of Dr. Bùi."

Melissa's father shrugged good-naturedly and adjusted his wireframe glasses. "Is Melissa there with you now?"

"Uh, she's at the library picking up her race packet," Beau lied. "I'm about to go meet her. I told her I'd call you to ask about the movie."

"Race packet?" Dr. Bùi looked confused.

"She's running the 5K, the fundraiser for the bee sanctuary tomorrow."

"The race!" The scientist looked like he'd suddenly remembered something. "I meant to tell her about the race, but I never did. How did she—"

"We saw a flyer at the library."

Melissa's father shook his head. "I see. I'm afraid I fit the description of an absent-minded professor."

"You're caught up in your work for the bees," Beau replied. "She loves to run, you know."

The scientist nodded. "That's something she and her mother always shared." He looked off to the side, silent for a moment, then turned back to Beau.

"Would you mind letting Melissa know I'm going to be pulling an all-nighter at the lab? I made a rather startling discovery this afternoon."

"Oh?"

"Against all odds, a few dozen of the missing Yolo bees have returned to the hive. But they're different; there's been a change."

Beau sensed a mounting excitement in Dr. Bùi's voice. "How do you mean?"

"Well, they're a bit larger, more robust. I'd swear even their faces seem happier, though I know that must sound ridiculous."

"Not at all. Melissa's been really worried about those bees. I think it's pretty cool how you and she rescued them."

Paul Bùi looked surprised, then grinned. "She told you about our bee heist?"

Beau grinned back. "Yeah, it was a big deal for her, you letting her help."

"Huh." The scientist adjusted his glasses and ran a hand through his hair.

"So, do you know where the bees went in the first place?"

Dr. Bùi rubbed his fingers through his hair and shook his head. "Not a clue. I'm examining some of the pollen they brought back to figure out where they've been, but the weird thing is, so far the pollen comes from plants that don't grow around here. I'm going to run some DNA tests on both bees and pollen."

"I'm sure you'll figure it out, sir." To Beau's dismay, Hermes started to whine in the background, but Melissa's father didn't seem to notice.

"Thanks, Beau."

Beau turned off the holo-screen and whistled. How lucky was that? He had the entire night to get Melissa back even though he knew there was nothing he could actually do except wait and hope she materialized before morning. If she didn't, well, he'd have to deal with the consequences of his lying as well as losing her. First things first. He decided to take Hermes back to Melissa's house, knowing the feisty lab-terrier must be famished, but Hermes' legs seemed to have grown roots that planted him to the ground. He would not budge.

Beau slumped down beside him. "You're a loyal one. I doubt Amaltheia would hang around this long if I vanished." He rubbed the dog behind the ears. Suddenly, Hermes pricked his ears upright and began to howl again.

"What is it, boy? What is it?"

The dog uprooted his legs and dashed around the tree several times, his short blunt tail straight out behind him. The air started to shimmer, followed by a golden glow, and then pop! there sat Melissa in the exact same spot she had been before she vanished. She looked dazed; her hair was mussed and her clothes crumpled as if she'd slept on the ground. Her right hand was curled in a soft fist. When she opened it, several honeybees flew out and made a beeline in the direction of the lavender field.

"Mel!" Beau shouted. "Where were you? I was worried sick. Are you okay?"

Melissa warily stretched her arms and legs as if testing whether or not they were really there.

"I was there and not there," she said in a low voice.

"What do you mean?"

"You know how Bella said quarks and gluons make things cohere so they seem solid?"

"Yeah?"

"Well, I stopped cohering."

Melissa squeezed Beau's hands as if to convince herself she was back in the solid world. She tapped her feet on the ground and shook her head. "I didn't know if I was ever going to get back."

"Were you in Dia?"

"Oh, Beau, I saw Karpos attack Amethea but I couldn't do anything. I was there and not there at the same time. And then later when she was sleeping, I melted into this light—I don't know how to explain it—and suddenly the light was a swarm of honeybees dancing around Amethea. I was dancing in the bodies of bees, Beau. Dissolved into dancing bees."

Beau looked at her in wonder. "I want to hear everything. But first, are you sure you're okay?"

"I think so. Nothing hurts. I feel like me."

"Good, because while you were out, I became the biggest liar in the county."

Hermes squirmed his way onto Melissa's lap and began covering her face in dog kisses.

"I'm glad to see you, too, Hermes!"

"Hermes wouldn't leave this spot. He was determined to wait for you."

Melissa kissed the top of the dog's head. "Amethea has a faithful dog, too. And Beau, Pythagoras was there."

"Pythagoras?!"

"He was fiddling with a piece of origami paper, trying to fold it into a bee! That was the last thing I saw before poof! I was back here."

They rode their bikes back to Melissa's house, and Beau insisted Melissa relax on the porch swing while he pulled potato salad from the fridge, made some peanut butter sandwiches, and brewed a pot of lemongrass tea. While they ate, he plied her with questions about her adventure.

"Pythagoras convinced the Dia Council to let Amethea run a race. She'll be able to do it now that her ankle is healed. It's the only chance Hippasus has."

"If she's anything like you, she'll win," Beau said.

"I'm sure she's way faster than I am, but she has to race the fastest boy on the island."

Beau took out his ball of modeling clay and mock tossed it. "Too bad she doesn't have a few golden apples."

"Maybe she has something better. The bees."

"Mel, I don't want you to ever disappear again."

Melissa placed her tea mug down. "It's funny, Beau. I've never felt so scared or so calm all at the same time. Somehow, it felt completely normal to dissolve into light, to turn into a swarm of bees. But another part of me didn't know if I'd ever get back home. If I'd ever see you or Ba or Noi again."

She reached for Beau's hand. That was the best feeling in the world right now, her solid hand resting solidly in his. Then she stood up and walked to the edge of the porch to look up at the night sky. She found the constellation Regulus and pointed out the bright blue star of the lion's heart to Beau.

"Amethea has the heart of a lion," she said.

"Or maybe a honeybee," said Beau. "By the way, your father said to tell you he'd be at the lab all night."

"That's nothing new."

"He said a few of the bees came back, Mel."

"They did?!"

"He's trying to figure out where they went in the first place."

"Good luck with that," said Melissa in a drowsy voice.

Before an exhausted Melissa crawled into bed, she hovered a finger over her holo-band and brought up the image of Amethea's statue. "Run swiftly, my sister," she whispered. She wondered who had made the statue and whether it had been made to commemorate Amethea's race with Eucles. If so, did the palm frond mean Amethea had won her race and Hippasus was safe?

All night as he kept vigil by the injured Amethea, Pythagoras had chanted healing invocations, but by flickering lamplight he had also examined the square of origami paper from the unfolded bee he had taken from the shrine. He was fascinated by it. Over and over he examined the fold lines and the angles and polygons they created. Carefully, he tried to fold the paper square back into a bee but was unable to figure out the sequence of folds.

It was a puzzle and a challenge, but something deeper, too. He sensed that the folds mapped harmony and music no less than the lines between stars or the chords on a lyre's strings. The lines on the paper held the secret language of honeybees. The origami bee was a Number spilled from the mouth of Apollo. Or perhaps from the mouth of Apollo's sister Artemis. Pythagoras set himself to recreating that Number. It was a Number that might save the boy, he could see that. He was certain that if Hippasus lived, he would become his greatest student, one who would eventually surpass even Pythagoras in understanding.

And now as Hippasus was led into the waves, Pythagoras stood on shore and continued to work on the paper square. He sensed he was close to a solution. When the red ribbon dropped, Amethea and Eucles burst from the start line, one a sleek dolphin, the other a swift horse, but they were a blur at the corner of Pythagoras' eyes as he worked his fingers on the paper. Close now, very close.

Hecataeus held his breath and gripped his right hand in a tight fist as he watched Amethea leap forward from the start line. Dika opened her hands wide and murmured a prayer to Pan. Kimon looked up and saw Amethea's long hair, like flames, streaming behind her. The two youths were side by side for the length of the beach but as they turned to follow the rocky path that climbed to the island's summit, everyone could see that Eucles had gained on Amethea by a stride length, and then by two, then three. They disappeared around a bend in the path. Dika moaned. Hecataeus gripped his other fist. Kimon continued to shape his clay.

Thinking the ringing was her alarm, Melissa rolled over in bed and grumbled, but when she looked at the clock it was only four a.m., two hours before she'd intended to get ready for the seven a.m. race. She realized her holo-band was vibrating so she grabbed it off her bedside table and tapped it. Noi's face appeared.

"Noi?" she said groggily.

"I wasn't sure what time you'd be off to your race, so I decided to call early."

"It's even earlier for you, isn't it?"

"Yes, yes, but that makes no difference. I couldn't sleep."

"Is something the matter?"

Her grandmother pursed her lips. "I've been thinking about our last conversation. Are you still having seizures and hearing that flute?"

Though Melissa had spoken with her grandmother and told her about the 5K, she had avoided telling her anything about her travels to Dia. Perhaps because she was still half asleep, Melissa no longer felt a need to hide what was going on and she blurted, "They're more than seizures, Noi. I've been in touch with a boy from long ago. I've been travelling back to Ancient Crete and the bees Ba and I rescued have travelled with me."

Her grandmother did not look the least bit alarmed. There wasn't a trace of doubt in her eyes, and it was that unusual fact that jerked Melissa fully awake. She sat straight up in bed.

"Wait! You believe me, Noi?"

"Yes, I do, and I had a feeling something like that was going on."

"You did?!"

Her grandmother put her palms together as if to form a lotus bud. "Melissa, I've had experiences myself. Mechtild is more than a painting, you know."

"You mean you've travelled to thirteenth-century Germany?!" Melissa stared, open-mouthed, at her grandmother's dainty, heart-shaped face. Her grandmother stared back with black eyes quick and bright as a sparrow's.

"That's right, and I can tell you about it some other time, but right now I want to know about your travels."

When Melissa finished telling her grandmother about Hippasus and Amethea and the Yolo bees, the quilt artist kept silent as if carefully considering all her granddaughter had shared. At last, she said, "Little bee, there was another Mechtild who lived in the same monastery as the Mechtild of my painting and she was both a poet and a beekeeper. In fact, I've been speaking with her…"

Melissa looked at her grandmother in wonder.

"There is a poem of hers I feel I must share with you. It may help you race in a way that will help your Dia friends and the bees you and your Ba rescued. I have a strong feeling your race is an essential part of it all. You must run today with all that you are."

Melissa listened as Noi recited the short poem and then went over it with her line by line until she had it memorized:

A fish cannot drown in water,
A bird does not fall in air.
In the fire of creation,
God doesn't vanish:
The fire brightens.
Each creature God made
must live in its own true nature;
How could I resist my nature,
That lives for oneness with God?

"Noi, I've always been afraid of my seizures."

"I know. Afraid of blanking out forever, right?"

"Yes. Afraid of not finding my way back, like a bee whose brain is damaged."

"And now?"

"I'm not sure."

"Run with the poem."

"I will, Noi."

A grey light filtered into Melissa's room by the time she said good-bye to her grandmother. The early morning sky was banked in dark clouds and the air was weighted and damp. It's going to be like running in a sauna, thought Melissa, unless the clouds burst and then it will be like running in a cataract. Undiscouraged, she ate a bagel with peanut butter. Always peanut butter! Imagine a world with strawberry jam, she mused, then pushed the thought away. She brushed her teeth, put on a pair of blue running shorts and a purple sports bra, double tied the laces on her running shoes. She filled a water bottle.

Beau arrived a few minutes later with Amaltheia in tow. Melissa clipped a leash on Hermes, but before she could hand the leash to Beau, Hermes bounded down the porch steps to greet the blue-eyed goat, trailing his leash behind him. For one cheerful, confused moment, Beau, Hermes, and Amaltheia were a jumble of leash and legs.

"Thanks for bringing Hermes, Beau."

"We'll be at the finish line to cheer, bark, and maa. Did you manage to get any sleep?"

"Enough."

"Good, because one of my mammoth lies was that you're a monster who races better on no sleep."

Melissa laughed. "I'm going to jog down to the river to pick up my race bib. See you later!" She waved and was off.

When Melissa reached the river, her skin prickled as she walked past the cypress tree where she had disappeared the day before. She was suddenly filled with doubt. What if Amethea needed her? Instinctively she reached for her pocket to pull out a piece of origami paper, but the pocket in her race shorts was empty. Why hadn't she thought to bring any paper?

She turned to run back home when the librarian, sitting at a nearby table handing out race bibs, saw Melissa and called out, "The bibs are over here!" The woman, her silver hair pulled taut in a ponytail, was wearing a white t-shirt with the silkscreened image of a large tarantula. "Let's see what you've got," she said in her Texas drawl. "According to Beau, you're a regular speed demon!"

As the librarian handed her the bib, Melissa stared at the number. She could hardly believe her eyes. Four hundred ninety-six. The third perfect number. She had a sudden feeling that she was not alone. Obviously there were other runners milling about, but she could sense some other presence, someone august and wise. If Pythagoras had strolled up at that very moment in a pair of race shorts, she would not have been surprised.

Okay, she told herself. I need to focus. Here. Now. This race. She went over the lines of Mechtild's poem, her grandmother's gift. I can use it as a running mantra, she realized, to keep my strides even. *A fish cannot drown in water, a bird does not fall in air...* She took her place near the front of the runners.

CHAPTER EIGHTEEN

STRAWBERRIES

Amethea leapt over stones and roots, running hard but always a few strides behind Eucles. His pace was so smooth it was like he was swimming. After the first stade, she felt a pain in her ankle, the one she had injured, a throbbing that increased with each footfall but she did her best to ignore it. Red ribbons dangled from bushes to mark the trail and every few stades an individual stood who had been instructed by the Council to make sure neither runner cheated by taking a short-cut. By the tenth stade, Amethea's thighs burned and the pain in her ankle was like a twisting knife. But she didn't break stride.

Eucles reached the highest point of the island first, well ahead of her. He quickly glanced over his shoulder to see how far behind she was, then sped down the path on the other side. At the island's crest, Amethea had a wide view of the crystal blue sea, the sea that was swallowing her brother. Her breaths came in rapid, painful bursts. This part of the trail, remote from village dwellings and shops, was seldom used and was, in fact, not far from the Bee Goddess' shrine. That fact heartened Amethea, and as she pressed on a line of honeybees appeared from the direction of the shrine and flew overhead. One bee strayed from the rest and darted towards Amethea's throbbing ankle. It stung her. The brief shock of pain from the sting cascaded into a warm flow that removed the greater knife-like pain Amethea had been feeling. The bee venom served as medicine.

"Sacred Bee, I accept your gift. Let me now run as quick as a celestial steed!" She leaned forward to lengthen her stride. She narrowed Eucles' lead by a stride, then two, but she could not gain further on him as the trail plunged back towards shore.

Pythagoras was smiling. He had it figured out now and neatly made the first folds in the sequence he felt sure would re-create the bee. At that same moment, several thousand bees left the hollow tree by the shrine and crossed over Amethea, giving her courage. One bee gave its life. The bees sped over the island towards the sea, and passed over the heads of the crowd gathered to watch Hippasus drown. Dika looked up and saw them. She nudged Kimon but could not pull his attention away from the clay he molded. A young girl was taking shape in his skillful hands, a girl in the passionate act of running.

Hecataeus saw a sudden gold shimmer of light surround Hippasus and then watched it lift and dissolve into the clear blue sky. The water had risen from Hippasus' waist to his chest. Hecataeus could see the boy's mouth was moving as if he were singing. On the wind he could barely make out the boy's words:

A fish cannot drown in water,
A bird does not fall in air...

Dr. Bùi was so puzzled by the DNA results he'd obtained by scraping a few cells from one of the returning bees and by the DNA from the pollen grains the same bee carried, that he went back to the field to check on the Yolo hive. The bees that had returned had to be from the original Yolo colony because otherwise the worker bees that remained with the queen would not have welcomed them back. And the DNA did match for the most part the strain of bees the Yolo bees belonged to but with a slight difference. They now carried a gene mutation that belonged to a honeybee that had gone extinct centuries before. The pollen grains matched pollen that his wife Claire had found in ancient Greek tombs. There was no way to explain it.

As Paul Bùi crossed the lavender field, thousands of bees suddenly popped out of thin air and made straight for the Yolo hive. He stood, mouth gaping and eyes wide, as every few minutes a thousand more bees appeared from nowhere. He pulled his glasses off to polish them three or four times because he had a hard time believing what he was seeing.

Running a race in Texas heat and humidity was tough, realized Melissa, as she pumped her arms and legs to carry her over the trail. Many runners appeared to have entered the 5K for a relaxing jog and several people were simply walking the trail, but others were giving it their all. Thoughts of Amethea inspired Melissa to pour on speed and one by one she began to reel in some of the fastest runners. She anchored the words of Mechtild's poem in her mind and found herself sending them mentally to Hippasus. He was the fish that could not drown, the bird that does not fall. *Live, Hippasus, live!* her mind called out to him. And then it was *I am running with you, Amethea!*

With each stride along the cypress-lined trail and beneath the cloud-darkened sky, Melissa found she was experiencing the meaning in each line of Mechtild's poem.

In the fire of creation,
God doesn't vanish:
The fire brightens.

Melissa had always feared her seizures, afraid her blank-outs would make her disappear, that she would cease to be. She now saw that was impossible. By accepting her seizures, she had touched the world of Amethea, become a golden swarm of honeybees. Become more truly who she was.

Each creature God made
must live in its own true nature;

She had hated her seizures but they were part of her nature, too. Every creature must be allowed to live its own true nature. That was why bee colonies had collapsed, why so many bees had perished. Humans had forced them to live against their honeybee natures, trucking them like prison crews to pollinate crop after crop after crop, never allowing them to rest or enjoy their own honey. And in doing so, humans had bent their own natures.

How could I resist my nature,
That lives for oneness with God?

How, indeed! Melissa ran even faster, enjoying the fact that she was a runner in a long line of girl runners, a line that she and Amethea both belonged to. And that was when she saw the swift, lean form of Amethea running alongside her, matching her stride for stride. As Melissa sped past cypress trees along the Sabinal River, she could smell the thyme-scented meadows of Dia. She was running in both worlds at once. She and Amethea ran as one.

Pythagoras' smile widened. Yes, he definitely understood the sequence of folds now. With each new fold he made, a thousand honeybees flew from the shrine's hollow tree, buzzed over the trail, and gave Amethea speed and courage. The bees dissolved over the turquoise sea and then popped out of thin air twenty-six hundred years into the future, to astonish an entomologist standing in a Texas lavender field. When Paul Bùi had recovered from his initial incredulous shock, he called Bella and when she joined him in the lavender field, a warm, rich laughter rose in her chest. She lifted her arms in the air as if they were wings and then wiggled and waggled in her own version of a honeybee dance.

Pythagoras was making the final fold just as Eucles and Amethea came tearing down the hill. He spread the origami bee's wings and the bee's legs dangled as if in flight. The final stade along the beach was all that remained and Amethea, to the crowd's astonishment, was only a stride length behind Eucles. The bodies of both young athletes gleamed like polished bronze.

Pythagoras blew on the origami bee and at that instant Amethea seemed to burst into flame. She felt the fire of creation in every cell of her body and knew her nature to be that of an athlete, no less than Atalanta. She gained on Eucles in the final seconds of the race and crossed the finish line a foot's length ahead of him. She staggered but did not fall, her eyes wildly searching the waves for Hippasus. The water had reached his chin. A wave crested over his head and he sputtered and coughed. He would choke on seawater!

Amethea shouted and pointed. Why was no one rushing to release him? She saw Karpos shove the man who had led Hippasus into the waves and helped tie him to the stake. In a flash she understood the same man was charged with releasing Hippasus should she win the race, but Karpos would not let him pass. While the two men argued, Hecataeus broke from the crowd and ran towards the water.

Pythagoras stood with his palm calmly raised to the sun. Origami bee four hundred ninety-six vibrated then lifted into the air.

Dika gasped and pointed overhead. More lines of honeybees, undulating and sparkling, had appeared in the sky. When Pythagoras released his bee, the others swooped down and followed it. They circled the crowd, zigzagged over the water, and hovered momentarily over Hippasus before flying high into the sky and vanishing.

"By the grace of Pan," Dika uttered. Kimon held a clay figure in his hand, a miniature version of a victorious Amethea.

Someone pressed a palm frond into Amethea's hand but she dropped it and flung herself into the sea to try to reach Hippasus. But her ankle gave beneath her and she collapsed. Her legs had no more to give. Someone in the crowd dragged her back onto the beach. Eucles, she now saw, had plunged into the shallow waters and swift as a dolphin swam to Hippasus. He and Hecataeus reached the boy at the same time and together broke the ties that bound the goat boy to the stake. Eucles carried Hippasus in his arms back to shore. When he lay the coughing, sputtering boy in Amethea's wet lap, he said in a low voice, "Forgive me."

"But you saved Hippasus from drowning!"

"I didn't slow my pace for you, Amethea. I intended to win."

Dr. Bùi cycled like a mad man from campus to the riverbank. He was determined to get to the finish line before Melissa crossed it. His conversation with Beau the evening before had triggered something inside him, and he'd thought about Melissa all night as he ran tests on the bees and pollen. Then, when he'd found something perched on a stone by the hive, thought turned to action.

As the overall winner of the 5K dashed across the finish line, Beau whooped, Hermes yapped, and Amaltheia gave a dainty bleat to celebrate Melissa's accomplishment. She was shocked to see her father, his face red and straining, running towards her.

"Ba, what's happened?"

"You," he said with a laugh and lifted her off the ground in a big hug. "High time I made one of your races."

Claps of thunder and the sudden pelt of rain quickly drowned out their voices. The librarian hurriedly placed a medal around Melissa's neck as everyone else rushed to gather belongings and head for home.

"That's quite a runner you've got for a daughter," she shouted.

"She's quite a daughter, period," said Melissa's father. They were wet as otters. Melissa was a stream of sweat and rain and tears.

"That's my Honeybee!" her father said, then caught himself, "Darn, I used it again."

"Ba, it's okay. Honeybee works.' Melissa smiled and wrapped her wet arms around his neck.

After everyone had a chance to dry off and change, Beau and his mothers joined Melissa and her father on the Bui's covered porch for a post-race brunch. Rain fell in steady silvery sheets and the wet earth released a rich, spicy aroma. Bella brewed a pot of mint tea and Rocio surprised everyone with a big bowl of fresh strawberries.

"Thanks to the steady increase of sanctuary bees," she said, "neighbors are growing things they haven't been able to in ages. I swapped some goat cheese for these."

"Strawberries!" exclaimed Melissa. "I've always wanted to taste one." Rocio handed her the bowl and Melissa selected a plump one. Everyone watched as she took a bite.

"Oh my gosh," she said, "Ba, we need to grow a whole field of these!"

After everyone had eaten their fill, Beau and Melissa rocked on the porch swing. Beau was modeling a victory statue for Melissa based on the statue of Amethea that Claire Berry had discovered on Dia.

"I saw her, Beau, I saw Amethea. We ran the race together. Hippasus is safe."

Beau squeezed Melissa's hand, covering it in red clay. She smiled and didn't bother to wipe it off.

Her father and Bella couldn't get over the return of the Yolo honeybees and the inexplicable DNA results. "There's something quarky about the whole thing," Bella punned and they all laughed. "Seriously, though, we're getting close to figuring out how a quark communication system might work for honeybees. And when we do, we've got some questions for those Yolo bees."

Melissa's father adjusted his wire-rimmed glasses and ran his fingers through his black hair. "I'd really like to know where the bees went and how on earth they returned with altered DNA. They are now the healthiest, most robust honeybees I've ever seen. And the happiest."

Melissa stood up and went inside. When she came back out she was holding her basket of origami bees. She poured them out onto the porch table. 'Four hundred ninety-five," she said. "I counted them last night."

"Why, they're beautiful!" said Rocio.

"Four hundred ninety-six," corrected Dr. Bùi. He reached into his pocket and pulled out an origami bee. "I found this one on the large rock near the Yolo hive early this morning. I had no idea you'd been folding so many, Melissa."

Beau and Melissa looked at each other. "Your call, Mel."

"Beau helped. They were for you, Ba. We were going to fold a thousand as a kind of prayer for honeybees, but it turns out that four hundred ninety-six was the right number."

"I don't know what to say. They're beautiful, Mel. So much careful effort." Melissa's father was clearly moved.

"Hey, that was your race bib number, too, wasn't it?" asked Bella.

"The third perfect number," said Beau.

"Yeah, it was perfect," said Melissa. "In fact, it's the luckiest race bib I've ever had. It had a six in it and four times nine is thirty-six which, of course, is six squared, and six stands for hexagons, and honeybees are hexagon engineers. And—"

Beau lifted an eyebrow. "Mel, you are an incorrigible math geek."

Her father looked at her, his face bright with pride. "And?"

Beau incised a tiny bee on the heel of his statue of Melissa. "It's rather a long story, Dr. Bùi, but we've got all day, right?" He smiled at Melissa.

The adults stared at the two teens.

Melissa cleared her throat and began, "It all started when I heard a flute in the almond orchard the night we stole the Yolo bees..."

EPILOGUE

A small bronze, no more than eight inches tall, stood in an alcove of the shrine. It was a girl runner holding aloft a palm leaf. A gold votive of the Bee Goddess stood on a polished block of rose-colored marble at the shrine's center. When no one else died of fever after the race between Amethea and Eucles, several families donated stones, tiles, and labor, and under Kimon's direction, restored the ancient shrine.

A red-haired woman stood with her young daughter and offered an armful of white roses and barley cakes to the Goddess. A few honeybees with folded wings rested on the altar stone. If you could read the faces of bees, you would have said these bees were happy and optimistic.

"Lay your flowers on the stone, Melissa," the woman said to the child. The small girl reached up and placed her wildflowers next to the gold votive.

The mother's hair was held in place by a circlet woven from green and gold threads. It was her favorite ornament, a gift from an admirer who later became her husband. He had given it to her after her victory at the Heraea Games the same summer the goat boy sailed with Pythagoras in search of Hyperborea.

When the mother and daughter exited the shrine, a man met them who tousled the child's hair and offered the woman a pomegranate. His warm skin smelled of apples and olive oil.

The child looked up at him and said, "Mother has been telling me the story of Atalanta."

"Has she? I will tell you an even better story."

"Eucles," demurred the woman, but he smiled and continued.

"A story about a woman from Dia who won a race with the help of magic bees."

The child's eyes danced. "What was her name?"

"Amethea," he answered, "Your mother, Amethea."

ACKNOWLEDGEMENTS

Deep thanks are due Sheila Black, Diane Gonzales Bertrand, Marisol Cortez, Cyra Dumitru, and Eliza Hayse for generous offerings of time, support, and valuable feedback.

Special thanks to my daughter, Emily Han, for first suggesting origami might be a vehicle for time travel, and to my son, Bruce Ho, who never fails to ask good questions.

Heartfelt gratitude to members of the writers and artists group, Stone in the Stream/Roca en el Rio who write, paint, and photograph the natural world with curiosity and wonder, and who advocate tirelessly for environmental and climate justice. A special thanks to Lucia LaVilla-Havelin for the embroidered honeybee that sits on my personal altar.

Deep gratitude to my godmother, the artist Meinrad Craighead, for her inspiring images of women mystics, especially her painting of Mechtilde of Helfta that plays a role in the story.

The first seed for this novel began by reading an article in the November 1997 issue of Discovery magazine about a mathematician's speculation that honeybees might access the realm of quarks to create their waggle dances. Any errors in my take on this idea are entirely my own!

Finally, a shout out to scientists, mathematicians, citizen scientists, beekeepers, artists, poets, and caring humans everywhere who are working to understand and protect pollinators.